JUPITER FLASH

Kadambur
Chandran

INDIA • SINGAPORE • MALAYSIA

ISBN 979-8-89133-902-6

In crafting this narrative, it is imperative to clarify that this is a work of fiction. Any resemblance to actual persons, living or deceased, or events is entirely coincidental. The characters, incidents, and locales portrayed in this book are products of the author's imagination. Any similarities to real individuals or occurrences are purely incidental. This disclaimer serves as a reminder that the primary purpose of this work is creative expression, and any unintentional resemblances to the real world are unintended and inconsequential.

Contents

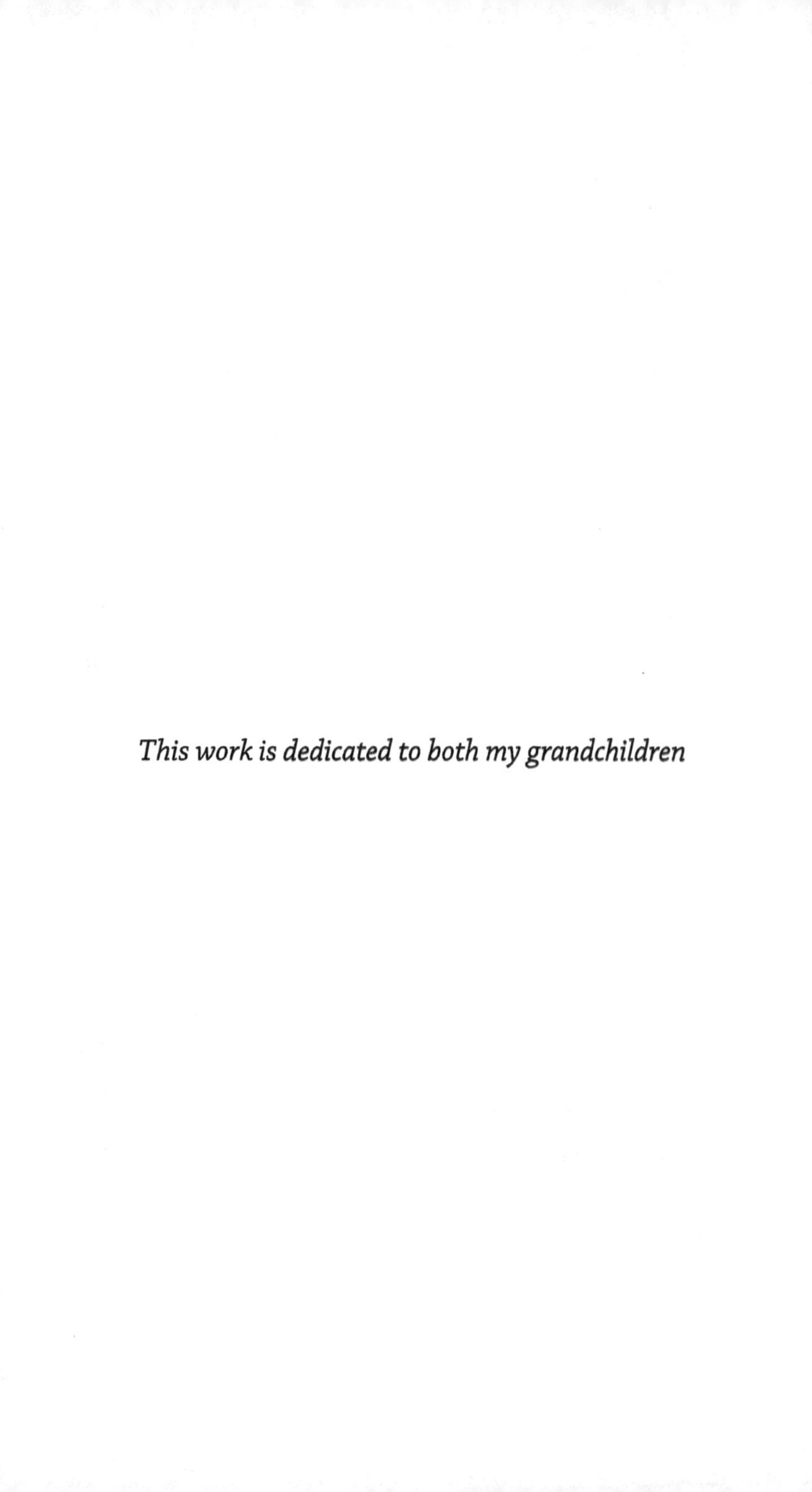

This work is dedicated to both my grandchildren

Prologue

A huge thunder broke the skies… a cloudburst sort of thing… whole area was shaking like a leaf… torrential rains poured non-stop…Narayanan knew it was a landslide… their house was strong and was not very near any river… but this!!! Ammu, his eight year old daughter hugged him, scared to the bones… Gopu his 12 year old son was trying to pacify his mother Rathnam and his 80 +grandfather. Suddenly there was a thud!… he felt the land moving…slowly, then the speed increased… all of them cried aloud… darkness! Darkness! He opened his eyes after sometime and could see that he was on an island which was floating… there were few other neighboring houses too… they floated and floated… sometime in the dark… sometime in hazy light… wind blowing at high speeds… no one dared to get out of the house… it must have been a few days…months… they had lost consciousness… when he woke up, the atmosphere was calm……rain was a drizzle, wind was more of a breeze and they were moving slowly. He looked at his family, all were intact; He prostrated in front of the small statue of Krishna kept at the 'Sivothi' and said, "Krishna, you saved us". He opened the door.

He couldn't believe what he saw!… there were a number of huge floating islands coming together and clashing with each other creating hills and crevices… he looked dumbfounded in astonishment and bewilderment…!!!

It took few more days for the newfound collection of islands to stabilize into one piece of land. He stood outside his broken door and looked across to another man standing on a broken wall… "hullow!" The man turned towards him and with a look of relief and surprise shouted, "haaai! Any idea where we are?"

Small pieces of land from various continents have floated and formed together to form a huge island as big, or bigger than Australia!

Narayanan replied with a thrill,

"Yes my friend, we are… NOWHERE!!"

CHAPTER 1

Vaikunta (The Reign of Vishnu)

Vishnu was ever calm. He was the master of the universe which included all the galaxies, solar systems and other stars. He could adopt any form, shape, visible, invisible... nothing was impossible for Him. He was the director and author of all the drama anywhere and everywhere in the universe. He was not bound by time as He himself was time!

He had evolved himself into three forms – Vishnu, Bhrahma and Rudra with Lakshmi, Saraswathy and Parvathy as their spouses respectively. Vishnu stayed in Vaikuntam, Bhrahma in Brhmalok and Rudra in Kailas. For the last so many earthly years (the span of an earthly year was a miniscule portion of a cosmic year) the solar system ruled by Aditya had been selected as the stage where life formed, lived and perished.

It was a huge hall where the atmosphere always remained most congenial. There were few others other than the three and their spouses in the hall. They were never visible for anyone other than those whom they wished to see. Certain exceptions were there. Narada, the observer of the universe was one such.

"Narada appears to be a bit concerned" said Lakshmi. "What's it Narada?"

Narada was ageless like the rest of them. He was omnipresent and knew what is going on in any part of the universe at any time. He has a veena which he could play extremely well. He used it to sing praises of any of the three or the one Superior to them. There was only one person who beat him in music... Hanuman who had filled his mind with seamless devotion. Narada spoke in a sweet voice.

"There is unrest between Aditya and Bruha. Bruha feels that Aditya has been partial to Pritha and Mangal. This is disturbing the tranquility of Suryaloka."

"Why so?"

"Bruha being the second most important chief in Aditya's realm he wanted to host the living world in his empire. But you know, Aditya goes by the rules and he gave it to Pritha as per the schedule. Mangal is next in line and thereafter Bruha. Bruha does not approve it."

Though Vishnu was aware of it all he allowed Narada to continue for the benefit of others. Narada continued,

"In his frustration Bruha bullied both Prithvi and Mangal. In that covert operation Parthivas, Pritha's husband was killed by Pushkara, one of the allies of Bruha. Though Bruha never wanted it... what is done is done. But unlike what Bruha expected, Pritha did not allow her realm to fall back. On the contrary she fought back and gave a stunning blow to Pushkara. The lady has, since then, been ruling most admirably well. Aditya do have a soft corner for her".

"That's interesting!"

"Moreover Pritha and Mangal both have already complained to Aditya about the incident and Aditya has called the council to decide on the punishment to Bruha."

"That is expected" said Maheswara.

"Yes, but Bruha... he is not happy with it. He plans to leave the Yootha"

"Nothing new... such things happen here and there often. It is Aditya's Yootham and he is immensely capable of managing it." The discussion continued for a while.

Narada mused and said, "In fact since Pritha became the ruler her realm is doing much better, her species also have been doing well. They are now in the last yuga and Aditya does not want any untoward incident to happen... however Bruha is in no mood to listen... ! I learn that he plans to smash both Prithvi and Mangal when he leaves, so that he is no more in Aditya's control."

"Let Aditya and his chiefs look after that and I am sure he will..." said Vishnu with a calm smile.

"Yet" Narada continued "you have always sent some part of your spirit to restore order. I think it is time...

you consider sending some of your force to the species in Prithvi"

Vishnu looked at others. They seemed to concede to Narad's opinion. He smiled benevolently and said, "So be it, but with a difference. This time it won't be a single life form like Vamana or Rama. It will be many from time to time till the end of Prithvi's span of life. The name will be... Kalki."

They asked Narada to inform in time, so that if any action needed from the side of the Trimurthys can be taken. Such thing used to happen in the universe earlier also. Since preservation was the duty of Vishnu he used to take incarnation and restore peace.

On earth it was few million years.

SOORYALOKA

It was brilliance all over. The vast palace, its grounds and the council halls were all bright and beautiful. The pillars were beautifully carved and inlaid with precious stones. Viswakarma, the divine architect have not spared any pains to make it as unique as his other creations.

Aditya paced the hall with unease. It was the fourth yuga as per their calender. Aditya was the emperor of this Yootham called Sourayootham. He was immensely powerful almost invincible. He had several gruhas under him with their peculiar physical characteristics. The

Gruhadhipathys included his own son and one woman who had to take charge due to the untimely death of her husband. The most powerful among his Gruhadhipathys was Bruha. He used to be a very knowledgeable and able ruler who wielded his power well. However, due to the greed of his subordinate commanders he had become cantankerous. Every such Yootha had their own schedule of events. Anyone who do not obey the schedule is cautioned, then punished and if required destroyed. The yoothas maintained order in that manner. Two of Adityas Gruhadhipathys began to show demonic tendencies few Souravarsha ago. Aditya was initially patient and tried to counsel them. However they took it for weakness and increased their trouble making. Finally Aditya destroyed them both and from the shattered pieces made a new Gruha and allotted it a place near Sani, his son. Bruha too was now displaying some such negative tendencies. He had a quarrel with Prithivas the ruler of Prithvi and in the milieu Prithivas was killed by Pushkara, a chief of Bruha. It is then that Pritha took over the reins and fought back. She almost killed Pushkara and Jaraya who were attacking her. Jaraya escaped from her somehow but Pushkara was taken prisoner. Bruha had to request her himself to release Pushkara who was shattered and bruised. She gave him on an assuarance that Bruha will not trouble Prithvi anymore. As per the schedule of Sourayootha, Prithvi had the chance to host species and next in turn was Mangal. Bruha, being the most powerful wanted the species for his Gruha before them. This was the bane of contention between them.

"You have given the species to Pritha while I am the seniormost and most powerful Gruhadhipathy under you"

"C'mon Bruha, you know that things here are done as per the order. The order was made long back. Two of our Gruhas already hosted them and now it is Prithvi's turn. So, you have to wait for your turn."

"I am the largest, Pritha is a female and Mangal is too small"

"It has got nothing to do with size, power, etc". Aditya's voice was firm, tough and soft. "The realm has a system and order, all should abide by it. In any case you will take time to prepare your Gruha for hosting species"

Bruha reluctantly agreed as he had not attained that much power, nor was his terrain prepared for hosting any species. Back in his Gruha he conferred with his 40 odd chiefs. They were of the opinion that he should go out of this yootha and make one of his own. He knew that Aditya will never stop him. However, for that he needed more time. In the meanwhile he wanted to give a scare to both Pritha and Mangal. Pushkara volunteered to go against Pritha while Genemendan was deputed towards Mangal. Pushkara created huge tremors and floods with an aim to destabilize the geographical structure of her Gruha. But she foresaw his intention and once again defeated him. Mangal also managed to ward off the threat from Genemendan with minor injuries. However both of them reported the matter to Aditya. Aditya was now furious and called for the full council.

The council hall was full. All his Gruhadhipathys (heads of states) were present. Bruha was huge by size and stature as much like Aditya except for the power and brilliance. Sani too was big and his black attire made him look menacing. All the twelve of them were special by their characteristic status. The one and only female chief Pritha, was simply outstanding. She was dazzlingly beautiful, elegant and gracefully ferocious. She exuded an aura of power which everyone admired except of course... Bruha and his chief, Pushkara. Bruha avoided Pritha though she paid her respects to him.

Aditya and Chaaya Devi arrived with accompaniment of music and drums. He was tall and excellently shaped like a carved figure. His dress was of golden hue and the spectre in his hand reflected all colours of the rainbow. He walked with a grand gate and sat in the judgement chair. Chaaya Devi sat behind in the Upasthanam (something similar to an adjudicator). After the mutual welfare enquiries done Aditya looked at his Guru for permission to begin the issue. Aditya's Manthrimukya (prime minister) rose and said,

"On behalf of Bhagavan Aditya I welcome you all to Sooryaloka. We have a complaint from Pritha and Mangal against Bruha which you are all aware of." He briefly gave the details of the complaint including the death of Prithivas. "Arya Bruha, would you like to say anything?"

"Well…" Bruha rose and said with his usual drawl. "It was more of an accident… I deeply regret the death of Arya Parthivas."

"Huh!… an accident?" Pritha asked? "Pushkara killed my husband by deceit and not even a fair fight,… and Arya Bruha, you call it an accident!?"

There was a roar of approval from the assembly. Bruha was angry and yet, controlled. He said, "I have been insulted here and therefore I would not like to continue in this Yootha"

"No one has insulted you" said Aditya. We have a schedule and it does not differentiate between size and stature. You have to wait for your turn. I have told you this earlier also. However that's no reason for your attacking Mangal and Pritha"

Bruha knew that he was at fault but he didn't care. In his mind he repeated 'I will get out of here… sooner, the better'.

The council debated the crime and finally the punishment was declared. Navadandana it was… nine strikes!

Bruha shouted in rage. "I will take it… for the last time. It is all because of Magal and Pritha… you will suffer… before I leave!"

"The choice is yours, Arya Bruha". Aditya said in a calm but firm voice. You are welcome to stay with us or move out on your own. But if you meddle with any of the Sourayootha I will not tolerate it. You know me well...!" The tone of Aditya was enough for all to know what it meant.

He had to accept it, for he knew the power of Aditya. Once Sani, despite being Aditya's son had tried to rebel; and he is still carrying the rings around his neck. On yet another occasion two others who were even stronger than Bruha had confronted Aditya. They were shattered and disappeared permanently. The scattered remains were accumulated later and made into a realm and allotted a place near Sani under Sushruvas.

"I know that Bhagavan Aditya" Bruha bowed in acceptance.

Bruha decided to take the punishment awarded by the council and try to get away from this yootha. He knew that Aditya will never stop him. Then he will create his own realm with all his 40 odd chiefs spreading out... Bruhayootha!

As he left the hall he looked straight into the eyes of Pritha. She never even wavered and looked back gracefully.

* * * * *

CHAPTER 2

The Past

Ujjain 117 BCE

Agnisarman could see the silhouette of the aashram from where he was sitting. The Kshipra river flowed near the aashram. He had come to the river bank to observe the sky. He forgot the time as he sat contemplating the placement of stars and constellations. He mumbled to himself, "Yes... it has to be" and with a sudden excitement dived into the river.

The Aashram of Varahamihira, the astrologer, scholar scientist of King Vikramaditya's court situated on the banks of Kshipra river. He was famous not only in Ujjain and Bharathvarsha but also in the Yavana country (Greece of today). He held discourses with scholars regularly in the illustrious court of the famous emperor. He was one among the 'Nine Jewells'. He had several students including one from Yavana Desam staying and learning in the ashram. Agnisarman was one of the most intelligent students whom Mihira had a special admiration. The young man used to think out of ordinary and it always led to something.

"So you mean to say" said Prithyusas mockingly, "that Guru gruha is likely to move out of this Sourayootha and create one of its own?"

All other students joined together in the laughter. They knew that Sarman has a habit of bringing up weird ideas... but this was too much!

"Prithyu brother, I am certain it will... I can prove it with my calculations!" Sarman was serious. The group debated the matter cracking jokes at Sarman; at the same time Sarman trying to defend himself with his arguments. As the debate became louder Mihira came out of the ashram and joined them. All were quite now.

"So what was it all about?" he asked calmly.

"Father, Agnisarman has now brought up a theory that Guru Griha is likely to leave this Sourayootha...!" Prithyusas replied him respectfully. He was Mihira's son and the senior-most among them.

"Huh!" even Mihira was surprised but he didn't show it. "There must be a reason why Agnisarman thinks so... So let us have your theory Sarman" Mihira sat on the leopard skin spread on the raised ground under the baniyan tree.

Agnisarman was very happy. At least the teacher has not mocked him. He fanatically explained the positioning of planets and the relative differences between them. Thereafter he proceeded to the position of planets in a near future date... yet another... and yet another. He said,

"Guru is moving in a very awkward manner, he is closing towards Bhumi." Everyone including Mihira was aghast because at first look, the calculations were correct.

He continued, "At this rate, in a future time it will move away going through a path somewhere between Prithvi and Mangal! If it does so, it will almost hit Prithvi…and…!"

"Hold Sarman" said the teacher. Mihira looked at the calculations, closed his eyes and contemplated a while. "What you said does make sense. We need to carry out a detailed analysis."

He allotted two groups, one under his son and the other under Agnisarman to logically calculate, argue and come to a logical conclusion. He himself and the rest of them were to be observers. His daughter-in-law Khana who was as knowledgeable or more as any of them, was to be the adjudicator. They discussed and debated for three days before arriving at a conclusion.

It was –

'that Guru gruha will continue to move at an increased pace and will pass in between Bhumi and Mangal in some 1500 to 2000 years (somewhere in 21 century). There is a possibility that the incident may break Prithvi and Magal or push them into different orbits. As per the calculations they predicted that soon after Prithvi will begin to freez!'

Varahamihira heard them out patiently and felt that it needed deeper contemplation and analysis. He studied all the calculations all alone in his quarters a number of times. He was surprised to learn that this was a true possibility. He was highly impressed by his student Agni Sarman. He sat in meditation for a day contemplating on this and he could see it happening... a great calamity in a far future. He sent his son with a message to the chief of scholars of the palace seeking permission to present this discovery in the court so that all scholars may discuss it. The King and the think-tank were impressed and intrigued by the proposal and ordered the theory to be presented in the court.

On the day of the event Varahamihira prayed to Aditya in the morning. He invoked Sun in his mind and said, "Oh! Aditya, is it true that Bruhaspathi might leave your reign and start his own Yootha? The jyothirganitham indicates so. Please guide us correctly"

The court was full of scholarly people. The King himself was a great scholar and thinker. They were ever open to ideas from anywhere. Kalidasa the epic poet considered Mihira as the seniormost among the 'nine jwels' of the court. The King asked Varahamihira to present the strange theory for the consideration of the sabha and if needed to warn the future generations.

Varahamihira introduced the subject and allowed Agnisarman to explain it in detail to the assemblage of scholars, royals and public. The scholars and King listened to the presentation by Varaha Mihira and Agnisarman. The court debated the subject for further clarity though they could not reach any appropriate conclusion. One thing was certain that there is a huge possibility as per the prevailing astronomical knowledge. The king ordered the theory and its calculations to be recorded on scrolls and preserved properly for the future generations. It was done and the scrolls were sealed in a strong box and kept in the underground cellar in the Rajdhani.

Agnisarman said as if to himself, "I wish I could be there when it happens!!!"

"You never know" Varahamihira said with a smile.

Centuries later the famous Rajdhani and the sacred Sinhasan of Vikramaditya were destroyed in a natural calamity.

France 1552

The villa was luxurious as per the times. Salon-de-Province was a small commune located in the southern part of France, 52 km from Marseillis. Nostradamus had shifted here in 1547 only. He had been helping Dr Louis Serre in tackling a major plague outbreak in Marseillis for the last two years. Once it was tackled, he decided to settle down there as he felt very much at home in those quite surroundings. Anne and children were always there. He was a multifaceted personality –sometime doctor though he had no degree, astrologer, engineer and many more. Lately he had begun showing interest in predicting future. He used to go into a sort of trance and mumble continuously in bits and pieces which Anne used to scroll down in a sheet. Neither he nor Anne could make out much of its meanings. Since it had become a common occurrence he had kept writing material ready always for use. Anne was adept at writing down his mumblings.

It was a hectic day with the Queen Catherine de Medici. She had a fancy for him since he wrote all the horoscopes of the members of the Royal family. He relaxed in the garden. Anne and the children were moving around playing in the garden. Nostradamus was in a mood of romance. The spring brought the fragrance of flowers and myriad of colours in his garden. Anne sensed it and sat near her husband. He recited few lines of Michel Angelo's poetry to her to which she replied in Vittorio Colonna's lines. He was about to rise when the trance happened. Looking afar into nothingness he saw something. He spoke... "the giant... will leave. Burning ball of fire and gas... Will partially hit... huge crater... floods and thunder... rain torrential rain and winds... floating islands... forming new island... earth splitting and rising in huge clump as big as mount...500 to 600 years...new earth...covered in fog... beginning of the end..." he fainted. Anne had recorded the babblings as usual. She allowed him to rest a while. When he woke up Anne asked him about what he saw.

"I... I saw nothing!"

1993 CALIFORNIA, AMERICA

Professor Shoemaker, his wife Carolyne and his co scientist David Levy were thrilled.at what they saw. Shoemaker was a well-known personality due to his discoveries of craters, training of astronauts, association with moon missions and a variety of other scientific activities. Today they were observing something special through the 18 inch Shmidt camera at Palomar Observatory. They could find the presence of a comet like object orbiting Jupiter. On deeper analysis they found that this must have been in the orbit for 20 to 30 years. They called it SL9 (Shoemaker Levy 9). The discovery image gave the first hint that comet Shoemaker–Levy 9 was an unusual comet, as 'it appeared to show multiple nuclei in an elongated region about 50 arcseconds long and 10 arcseconds wide. Brian G. Marsden of the Central Bureau for Astronomical Telegrams noted that the comet lay only about 4 degrees from Jupiter as seen from Earth, and that although this could be a line-of-sight effect, its apparent motion in the sky suggested that the comet was physically close to the planet'.

The discovery spurred entire astronomical community all over the world to observe the comet. The calculations pointed to the course the comet was taking. It was expected to crash onto Jupiter in bits and pieces sometime in 1994. The collision was likely to open a small window into the giant Jupiter.

In June 1994 the entire world witnessed the cosmic drama for the first time. The first impact came at 20:13UTC on July 16 in Jupiter's southern hemisphere. This was detected by the instruments of Galeleo Spacecraft. Thereafter till 22 July it kept on happening. There were nine major impacts and many miner ones. The scars of the impact was seen on the planet for many months. NASA had collected all the data from all the observatories, Hubble, ROSAT, Ulysses and even from Voyager 2 which was on its way out of the solar system. The scientific community world over studied the impact and its after effects continuously. In 2009, July yet another black spot the size of Pacific ocean was seen on Jupiter, another comet or an asteroid probably.

...

India ISRO

Dr Kapilananda clicked a password and opened his PC. The screen displayed many lists of figures and notes. He had Kalam, Devyani and Misra as his audience. All of them were scientists working in ISRO. Kapil was an authority on scriptures and ancient history. Kapil said looking away from the monitor. "The earth was formed millions of years ago as per scriptures as well as science. Thereafter, Vishnu had a number of incarnations over the yugas. Scientifically life started and progressed, developed, continents were formed and populated... you know the story. Now we are in Kaliyauga and after a few thousands of years, earth will be no more. Scripturally, earth will go into Mahapralaya and will remain dead for eons!"

"We know all this... then?" Misra asked.

"Well, when the earth is inert the process of creation will happen elsewhere... may be Mars... Jupiter... Or any other."

"Hmm, that gives a lot of scope for our Underground City Project and Planetary Colonisation. Even the government is going strong on it." Said Kalam.

"Why not? The US, Russia and few other countries had a head start... we started to do so only in the 21st century. No government of the old..."

"Leave the creeping, Kapil... look ahead not back!" Devyani said.

Though the governments didn't put in much sincere effort the scientists of the country had collected together on a seemingly informal annual get-together. Without alerting the government they had formed a core committee to decide on the future environment for India. That was the birth of a secret project called "VYAAPTHI". It consisted of colonisation of space, other planets and even any inhabitable asteroids and designing of underground cities. They were so sure that one day the government will wake up and at that time, they should not fail the people of India. After all they were the devotees of Sarabhai, Bhabha and Kalam. This is the reason why, when the government at last woke up during the early 21st century the scientific community got a big boost for all their ventures. The country made its own cryogenic engine, satellites, PSLVs, Lunar and Mars missions, manned and unmanned space stations underground cities... all in a fast paced manner.

"You are right... I think we must concentrate more on colonisation than on underground living"

"Why so?"

"Because" said Misra, "the earth will take much more time to freeze, may be few thousand years. So we still have time to develop it"

"You have a point "said Kapil. "I feel Kalam and Devyani should direct their attention towards space while Misra and self will work on the Underground cities"

* * * *

CHAPTER 3

Present

2035 ISRO India

He languished in the convertible chair closing his eyes. The atmosphere in the room…rather laboratory was pleasant except for the whirring of the AC. They thought that he was sleeping being awake for the last so many hours. But then, for him once the work starts sleep and rest were secondary. 'Kalaam'… that was the name with which he was known. He had adopted it due to his obsessive admiration to the Late Abdul Kalam, the Missile Man of India. Otherwise he was Devdut Bhatt an engineer from Aligarh University who took up and excelled in Nuclear Physics. He was somewhat a loner but ever brimming with energy. His knowledge about anything and everything under the sun was phenomenal. It was he who created India's first manned Space Station Thrisanku. Devyani was looking at the screen with full concentration. She raised her eyes and glanced towards the languishing form with surprise in her eyes.

"Kalaam, what are you dreaming"?

Devyani was the Mission Commander of THRISANKU a part of 'J QUEST'. It was a universal outlandish project in which all the world was participating. India was the leader because Dr. Kalaam was the originator of the project. Though initially the world especially NASA, China and the Arab world called it a bizarre dream of a maverick scientist gradually they understood that it was neither bizarre nor dream but a looming reality which was about to happen! The main project was given a Sanskrit name THRAANANAM (Rescue). J Quest was part of that program.

"I am visualizing C'men with his hip flask and you with the command look coping to each other in the 'Valley of New Life'

"C'mon Kalaam, I thought you were thinking of Maya". Maya was Kalaam's unwed wife.

"Maya! yah." Kalam sat upright slowly and smiled. "I can't dream of her because…, she is always here" he thumped his chest. He nursed the Shivas Regal slowly. Devyani's mobile made a donkey cry… C'men.

"Ha!" she said to it and then turned to Kalam. "He is waiting with fresh hot biriyani and parotta and of course pappadam. Let us have it".

Dr. Devyani, C'men (short for Col Chandran Menon) and Dr. Kalaam were good company. Kalam was a maverick scientist while the other two were astronauts cum scientists.

It was September 2030 on Earth. The converted laboratory cum observatory cum control room looked more like the Master Room of some sci-fi movie. Kalam was the head scientist of the project while Dr.Devyani was the Chief of Mission and C'men, her husband was the chief of Staff.

Dr Devyani Chandran was in her early forties, good looking and extremely energetic. She was one of India's top space scientists with many degrees, awards and rich experience of space travel. Since the launching of the mission she was the obvious choice of Head of the mission. She had launched satellites, travelled to space stations of India, NASA and certain other countries and had many hours of space walk. She had rescued two ships one of USA and another of Russia, had boarded and repaired a stricken spaceship of Germany... all in space! In the international space circle she was known as 'Angel/Devi'. In space, the world was one... all helping each other.

From the beginning of 21st century India had accelerated her progress in space exploration. They had established manned space stations in Moon, one beyond Mars and yet another. There were few other stations too; some of NASA, Russia, Germany and so on. In addition observatories like Hubbles had also been stationed at different areas. Some of them which were initially unmanned and stationary, had since been manned and made mobile. All of them shared data with each other as per the **UN Space Protocol**. Few countries including India had achieved the capability of space travel. From 2020 onwards the space travel had become a tourist attraction. The technology steadily progressed, inventions happened and the speed and volume of space travel had gone up. India was in the elite group of countries which had established joint ventures in Moon, Mars, and few locations in the outer-space. She also had two independent space stations from where they could taxi around in manned space modules for outer-space exploration. The fuel for the ships were taken from the space itself which was in abundance. The advantage was that India was the only country which had the knowhow to extract fuel from space. India had also acquired the capability to travel almost at the speed of light. This was done by a process called "IAT (Identifiable Atomic Transformation)". An entire spaceship with its crew and equipment could be transformed into 'identifiable groups of atoms and mounted on a light frequency, travel with the light ray to the target and on reaching the target the grouped atoms were transferred back into its original manifestation. It used nanotechnology combined with atomic science. In this sphere also India was far ahead of other countries. In short India had become the leader of Galactic exploration.

The progress of the country had created some initial problems internally as well as externally. However, the Indian military and DRDO had outgrown the government and political control due to the dedication and integrity of its officers, soldiers and other employees including scientists and research fellows. They had learned to circumvent the bureaucratic injunctions and political manoeuvrings and had produced an array of secret weaponry unknown to the outside world. Missiles like Brahmos were the initial ones which were showcased so that the world was made to believe that this is all that India had. In fact she had far superior weapon system, invisible stealth bombers, shadow fighter aircrafts, precision ICBMs that could carry any type of warhead anywhere in the world, submarines with extreme capabilities- manned and unmanned, robot controlled aircrafts, space weapons and most importantly, 'Tomorrow Weapons' which were a group of ground operated or spacecraft operated weapons from space; silent and invisible! Some of them were used in the three front war they had in the mid21st century. That established India as the most powerful nation, economically, militarily and scientifically.

ISRO, VSLC, DRDO and the IITs were in the thick of it. While the scientists like Kalam, Devyani and a host of others researched and visualised the future scientific environment for the country and the world, some of these data were shared with other nations also. The government had expanded Hindustan Aeronautics Limited into the premier Aircraft and Spacecraft builders. It had several subsidiaries located at different parts of the country.

Huge effort had been employed in 'Tomorrow Science'. This was centred round study of goings on in regions outside the earth's periphery in outer-space all the way to the periphery of the solar system and within the earth as the world felt that the earth would soon go into a deep cold winter. India had recorded a number of small and big black holes, galactic winds, hospitable areas in certain other planets, and a variety of such other features in the outer-space at the same time identifying and preparing underground laboratories, cities and the like taking a cue from the ancient history of the country. From the novices of the 1950s India had become the foremost explorer of Outer-space, Nuclear science, Inner core and a variety of other scientific fields. India, no more imported technology but exported it at a reasonable cost.

The Space Forum was an annual event held in one of the five countries – India, USA, Japan, Germany and Russia under the aegis of UNO. Since these five countries and a few other countries had started their own manned/ unmanned space stations UNO had entered the picture to regulate the traffic and proliferation in space. The UNO had taken a lot of criticism in their handling of Covid 19. Thereafter, UNO was reorganised with India also as the elected member of the five member committee. Individual Veto power was removed and a collective Veto of three members at the least was introduced. However there was no occasion where they had to use such a veto since their decisions became unanimous. UNO grew stronger with cooperation and understanding from most of the countries. A few rogue nations were still there but not of much consequence. The communal flare ups of the early 21st centuries had subsided thanks to the 'Global & Galaxial Welfare' document introduced by India during the late 21s and adopted by UN as the prime requirement for the future of earth and solar system. All space tourism was controlled and regulated by UN Space Adventure Organisation-UNSAO for short. Gradually the world was focussing more on space rather than earth. The UN Space Coordinating Committee-UNSCC became the apex body for all space related subjects.

UNO had also formed a committee to prepare the world for underground living. Most countries had created townships where a sizable population can survive. The World Science Forum had proclaimed that the earth will be gradually moving into a winter where the waters of the oceans will begin to freeze and oxygen will become scarce on the surface of earth. There were few pockets which were likely to retain the nature as it was. However they were also hanging in suspense because of the imposing cosmic events.

In 2015, the discovery of a new planet was announced by NASA and they named it Kepler 452 b. In the 20th century Dr Chandrasekhar, an Indian born scientist had created flutter by establishing the existence of black holes. is His contention was that these were not dwarfs but collapsed stars. New planets, black holes and many such other discoveries revolutionised the concept of Astrophysics. Gradually it was established that the new planets were actually not new but formed out of the debris of certain other planets 'collapsed' eons ago. The black holes still remained an enigma.

It was in the late 20th century that Shoemaker and Levy tracked a comet that was heading towards Jupiter.

The cosmic phenomenon was the first of its kind observed by the world. However, they forgot it immediately after, since world was busy with Lunar and Martian probes. The massive earthquake of Latur, India, series of quakes all over the world, the untimely floods, cloudbursts, tsunami and such other natural calamities were viewed as a result of shifting of tectonic plates and due to environmental damage caused by manmade efforts. Indian scriptures had predicted such events as the earth was in its last lap towards the delusion (Pralayam). Sages of the ancient had predicted such events, so did Nostradamus, Chinese philosophers, some astrologers from different parts of the world and a few scientists. The world never believed that Dinosaurs could exist but new discoveries proved their existence. Films like Jurassic Park was lapped up by the public as well as the scientists. Yet the knowledge about the cosmos was so limited that every day observatories were finding something new.

It was in the early part of 21st century that Kalam, then a student in IIT studying Space Science as a speciality, came up with a very strange theory... He had by accident, observed Jupiter. He felt that there was something happening in Jupiter which defied explanation. He decided to study it more in detail. He analysed all available data on Jupiter and the cosmic event of 1984. He found that Jupiter was having sudden shivers frequently as if it was having some internal explosions. Initially the intervals of such shivers were long, 2 to 4 months. However as time progressed the frequency between the shudders decreased to few weeks and then to few days! Moreover, he observed that Jupiter was moving erratically. Since no astronomer could give him any satisfactory explanation he delved into scriptures, astrology, Egyptian, Chinese and old Red Indian folklores, Nostradamus prediction and many such unorthodox sources. His passion bore fruit. He had his answers.

Kalam then asked Devyani Sen and some other colleagues to join the research. Devyani Sen and a small group of students worked overtime checking and rechecking the data offered by him in his theory and came to the conclusion that it was actually possible and in a few weeks the final thesis was prepared. Kalam was an ardent admirer of Dr APJ Abdul Kalam. The name Kalam was adopted by him out of the admiration to his original name Devendra Bhatt. However, since then he was known as Kalam. He presented his theory for the first time in the 'Strange Events' debate. This was the idea of one of its most dynamic directors, Dr Asit Sen who wanted the students to think out of the box and look into bizarre but logical theories. Some such discussions had evolved into concrete theories like the 'Tomorrow Weapons', 'Space Living', 'Deep Winter on Earth', etc. and lead to the establishment of an organisation called 'Bhavishya Bharat/Future India'. BB was the coordinating and executing think-tank for the future of India scientifically. It was headed by the best scientist of India, Dr JJ Sing popularly known as 'Khalsa'. He was also present to listen to Kalam.

Kalam was young, brilliant and with a conviction which was contagious. He began by the 1984 cosmic event shown in a video on the screen.

"We all know what happened then. However, somehow no one bothered to know what happened after that in Jupiter". He switched the video off and continued. "Since then Jupiter had had a number of internal explosions regularly. Some of them were so powerful that Jupiter had wavered from its position. As it suffered more tremors it formed a pattern. Jupiter has begun to move out of the orbit." There was a sudden gasp in the audience. He continued to justify his findings with the help of different events like volcanic eruptions, untimely tsunami, cloud burst, floods and such other natural calamities. "The planet is moving in an erratic manner generally heading towards a path between Earth and Mars!"

There was a pin drop silence... then exclamations! "Are you sure it's not a dream",... "c'mon Kalam it is weird", "Doomsayer!" When it all subdued, Kalam continued calmly. "I will now present you the data obtained from all the observatories in space". He showed the logical sequence and calculations which led his team to this startling discovery. Gradually as the discussion progressed the audience began to be convinced of the possibility... no, reality of the event!

Kalam spoke further. "You must have heard about Varahamihira the astronomer in the court of

Vikramaditya of Ujjain. A small box, slightly damaged box of copper was kept in the Government Museum of MP unopened. This was an undated item received during an accidental excavation somewhere in the twentieth century. We had opened it and studied it with the help of Sri Sadasivan Namboothiripad, the renowned Vedic scholar and Thanthrik from the Kanippayyur Mana of Kerala. It contained a parchment which states certain findings by one of Mihira's disciples named Agnisarman. The parchment says that Guru gruh, ie. Jupiter is likely to move away from the Saurayootha in future... a period corresponding to late 21st century as per the calculations!"

"WHAT!!!" gasped the assembled scientists, historians and astronomers.

"Yes, Namboodiripad did his own analysis and study of the document in detail and confirmed it. He further mentioned that the unnatural natural calamities occurred in the early 21st century and continuing now are also due to this". He allowed the audience to digest what he said. "Dr Devyani will take on now"

Devyani Sen was an impressive young scientist who had already created waves internationally with her startling papers on space science. She was in her late twenties, a licensed pilot who could fly anything from a chopper to a sophisticated fighter jet. Then she was preparing for space travel. She was one of the recruits for the manned Lunar Mission of ISRO.

"We searched world over for any cues to this phenomenon. Many unexplained occurrences all over the world had strengthened our conclusion. The famous sci-fi writer Alex Maxievich suggested us to study the Nostradamus predictions. Accordingly we dug into it. There were half torn pieces of the writings collected and kept in a separate box. In that we could get the following..." She switched the screen on. An array of illegible writings were seen on the screen. One could hardly make out the paragraph. As if to clear their doubt she said,

"It goes like this...

'the giant… will leave. Burning ball of fire and gas… Will partially hit… huge crater… floods and thunder… rain torrential rain and winds… floating islands… forming new island… earth splitting and rising in huge clump as big as mount…500 to 600 years…new earth…covered in fog… beginning of the end…'

The ball of fire is Jupiter... the period corresponds to this century... rest you can imagine. All this corroborates the beginning of exit of Jupiter from our solar system. And the time is not far... In another10 to 15 years!" There was a deathly silence in the room. "Thereafter, whether... we will be there... or not... is... a big question mark!"

It was as if a bomb had exploded in the center of the hall. IIT further held discussions and detailed analysis of the entire data in collaboration with a group of senior scientists for yet another four days with cross-checking data from observatories, referring to old Sanskrit texts, discussing with few of the country's best astrologers and a lot of other sources including folk tales! They never wanted to have any loose ends from their sides. Once the institution was convinced of the theory, they brought the government also into it. The space observatories and ISRO confirmed the data. JJ Sing advised the government that UN should be brought into picture since this is a global affair. The government agreed and decided to let the world know about this in case they were not aware. Moreover India was sure that to save the earth some superhuman effort will be necessary and that has to be from all over the world. The government decided to present the case in the Space Forum to be held soon in Geneva.

* * * * *

CHAPTER 4

The Debate

June was a warm month in Geneva. The UN Council of Global Security (UNGS) was formed during early twenties. During the early part of 21st century a large number of natural calamities occurred which were unpredictable. These continued to happen. There were news of UFO siting though not confirmed, from certain parts of the world. Certain strange psychological phenomena also was observed. The scientists and thinkers felt that something sinister is going to happen sooner or later to the earth. General thinking was all these are due to environmental deterioration caused by human intervention. However, few countries including India, Germany and Russia were of the opinion that the earth is approaching the end of its lifespan! They stated that the glaciers had already started melting, the oceans are rising, a number of small islands have been swallowed up by the sea, temperature extremities were bewildering, hectares and hectares of land were becoming barren- many such strange happenings. In their opinion the earth may become uninhabitable gradually..., may be in a few thousand years. That prompted the formation of UNGS. It was under their aegis, the underground cities, floating townships and plans to populate some planets, started.

UNGS comprised a member from each country. The apex body was the UNSC of five members including India headed by the UN Secretary General. The present SG, John Onkarabile was a well-known environmentalist, social activist and a man of immense knowledge. He had studied Sanskrit to read Indian scriptures and epics. Under him the world leaders had begun to cooperate for a common good.

The SG rose to address the members. "I welcome you to this august conference. The issue at hand is more diabolic than any the world have faced till date. Without going around preambles I invite India to present the issue."

Dr JJ Singh asked Kalam to proceed. Kalam rose and went to the podium. He moved the screen to the centre so that everyone can see it. His support staff had already made elaborate arrangements in the hall so that when required it could become a planetarium or a theatre. He was tall, good looking and radiating energy. His hair, as usual unkempt like that of a mischievous boy. He missed Devyani Sen since she was on honey moon with her maverick husband Col Chandra Mohan Menon popularly known as C'men. Well, the honeymoon was... in a space shuttle!

"Friends, probably we are the last generation who would see the earth like what we have seen..., the sky, the planets, the greenery, rocks and rivers...! In a few years all this is likely to disappear along with the inhabitants! The scientific evidence points to this. Though we have already created out-stations in the space, moon, etc, underground cities and floating islands and such other survival measures all this exists if",... he gave a meaningful pause and said... "WE exist!" Kalam elaborated on the cosmic event of 1984 and the vibration Jupiter had with that. He explained the Varahamihira document, Nostradamus prediction, India's investigation and conclusion, inputs from Germany, China, NASA, and few other countries. It took an hour and half of total absorption. He concluded, "So, in short Jupiter is likely to pass between Earth and Mars, either smashing them into pieces or sending them into some different orbit!"

There was a deathly silence in the hall. The SG spoke through his mike, "C'mon gentlemen shoot him with your questions"

There indeed were questions and questions. Kalam had all the answers. When the Forum concluded the entire world was generally convinced that this is going to happen. Now it was the turn of SG once again.

"So, we have the problem. Now I would like you to discuss the issue in your countries with whatever expertise you can get and meet again here..."

"In two months' time" Kalam interjected. "Sorry to interrupt Mr Secretary General, the time is at a premium".

"Do you have any solution, India?"

"Yes and not yet... but in two months... we will have."

John Onkerabile liked the confidence of Kalam, he smiled and said, "so be it...two months!"

COSMIC UNIVERSE

Bruha Loka

In the realm of Bruha the tempers were high. Bruha and his chiefs felt that 'Navdandana' was the biggest dishonour they had to suffer in Sourayootha. They blamed Pritha and Mangal for it. They had to take it because they knew the power of Aditya.

"That woman... Pritha!" Bruha roared... "she didn't even flinch, looked straight into my eyes... I hate her guts..."

"We must teach her a lesson Maharaj" Pushkara said with venom in his voice. He passed his hands involuntarily on the right side of his face... Pritha had slashed it...she could have killed him, but she didn't! He felt as if he has been 'branded' and spared for another day. "As we go, I will make sure that Prithvi will be shattered"

"I think you are right Pushkara... Plan accordingly. Let Genemendon deal with Mangal"

"My pleasure Bhagavan" Genemendon said.

"We will prepare to exit from this Yootha and make our own in the Palazhi itself." He further gave orders to his Mukhya Sachiv and Mukhya Senapathy to prepare for the deployment of forces and arrangements for move.

Duties were arranged to all the 40 odd petty chiefs of Bruha's realm to navigate out of the Sourayootham.

There are a number of 'Thamogarthams' enroute which are so powerful that they can suck an entire Gruha into it. Then there are dangerous 'Chakravaayu's which can push or divert a Gruha from its direction. They decided that on completion of preparations the time for move will be finalised by Bruha.

Prithvi

This was the first time Pritha assembled her council after the meeting at Aditya's palace. She was grace and elegance personified. Dressed in a blue and pink attire She looked more than the Empress she is. There was boldness in everything she did or spoke. She explained everything including the perceived nefarious intentions of Bruha.

"He is moving out all right... but as he leave he is likely to strike us and Mangal."

"How can we ward off Bruha?" her Mukhya Senaadhyaksh Vajra Simhan asked.

"Bruha will not hit us directly but he is most likely to depute that task to Pushkara.... may be some others too. You send your special people and try to find out that"

"I already have some leads Arye" Bhavani, the chief of her espionage organisation said. "Pushkara and Genemendan has been tasked to hit us from two sides. Their aim appears to be to split Prithvi into two. Some others have been tasked to do similar job on Mangal. Dheeman, the chara sachiva of Mangal is in contact with me."

"Ohh!" it was a collective exclamation of surprise and caution.

"You must be having some ideas, Bhavani"

"Yes, Aarye. I have identified two 'thamogartham' in the region. We should try to push Pushkara and Genemendan into them by deception"

"Excellent!"Pritha rose and pointed to a vaccum, it became a glass screen like thing where a part of the vast space was visible to all. She looked at Vajra Simha who rose and explained the path which Bruha is likely to take and the location of the thamogarthas en-route. He wanted Pushkara to be lured to expand his forces in such a manner that his periphery moves closer to the thamogartha. The excitement should be such that he should not notice it at all. "And at that moment we give him the real blow"

"He should be forced to fall back and that will make him move closer to the thamogartham and the rest will be done by it".

"If I may suggest Aarye" Heramba, her saasthrajna said. She was in charge of secret and improved weapons and other such affairs of the area of influence of Pritha in Paalaazhi. "I have designed two Chakravaakas big and small. We can make more too. These may be of use against Pushkara, Genemendan and even Bruha when he pass by us"

The action plan was discussed in detail and a general conclusion was drawn. The task was allotted to various chiefs, timings and the force to be used, to be given later. Vajra Simhan was to give the final order. Pritha called for next meeting within a short while. She dismissed the council except VajraSimhan, Bhavani and Thejaswini.

"Vajrasimha, you are aware of the information brought by Bhavani about our species. What is your opinion?"

Bhavani had observed the species for the first time accidentally. After the end of the Kurukshethra war the species had deteriorated for a while. Then their numbers started increasing and they spread all over the place and made different Dweepas. Gradually they evolved into seven of them. They inhabited five of them and started flourishing. This was the first time that the species occupied so much space. In a few days (centuries of earth's time) they became sophisticated emancipating from foot to horses to chariots drawn by horses then to chariots which were self- propelled. They travelled the seas and land on strange contraptions. Dwellings also increased. Flora and fauna flourished initially but gradually the humans started devouring everything. Then came the intelligent ones and the species became separated into different groups called Samrajyam. Eventually within another few days they started fighting each other like old times. Instead of the Chathuranga sena they were using different contraptions which could move fast, shoot projectiles with fire and certain other materials. The asthras and divyasthras were no more there. In their place they were using a variety of different weapons. Yet, they were advancing in life…!

They started travelling through the sky in something like a vimana and now they have begun to travel outside their periphery too. Their intelligence appeared to be growing very fast... they had started predicting... that too accurately about future which no previous species had done. Bhavani had seen all this and had reported to Vajrasimha.

"Yes Arye, since Bhavani told me their progress I too had observed them more closely. They are doing a fine job. They are even aware that we are going to close down soon. They have plans to colonise other Gruhas and Upagrahas also. Now to the latest sighting..."

Bhavani was passing an area between Prithvi and Chandraloka. She found a small chariot sort of thing rotating and landing on the barren area in Chandraloka! A door opened from it and something with a big coat and hood gingerly stepped out of it and walked a few steps. She was aghast and full of appreciation. Thereafter she found such vehicles at a number of places, some in which few humans and animals also were living!

"They have established a small home in the Chandraloka! This time the species are doing great"

"That's the point Vajrasimha,... the species are doing great" Pritha said appreciatively. "Why not we see them more closely and enhance their efforts?"

"What!!!" all the three of them gasped. Since the time Prithvi started hosting species they had never interfered with their evolution and progress. They have been flourishing for a few divine years and perishing and again a new set taking birth. The process had been going for ever but the Prithvisabha had never interfered ever. Why now?

"Yes! I am proud of them!" said Pritha. "We will incorporate their effort in our fight against Bruha." She knew there would be questions and doubts about such a consideration. "think over it and we will discuss in detail later. In the meantime I have a special task for Thejaswiny"

"My pleasure Arye"

"Find out the area south in Bruha's gruha... the one which he abandoned after the tussle with his sister... Deerghamandala. It is almost as big as Jambudweepa and inhabitable. I would like to colonise that area since he is not interested in it."

"That is a good plan" Vajrasimha said with admiration. Prithvi can later be joined with it!"

"You said it" said Pritha. "We will have to meet again soon!". She concluded the session and rose. All others too rose and bowed to her as she left the hall.

* * * * *

CHAPTER 5

J Quest – India

It was a few weeks after the conference at UN.

Kalam had already worked out a draft plan. From the available data they could draw the likely psth of Jupiter's exit. Most of the moons of the giant will pass harmlessly away from earth except for two... Io and Genymaede. Io can be diverted towards Blackhole M 32 and Genymaede can also be pushed away from harm. However the giant cannot be stopped or bypassed. Its magnetism would be so strong that when it passes it is likely to create a huge wedge on planet earth... something ten to fifteen time the size of Grand Canyon across the continents... it was likely to be in a zigzag pattern due to the rotation of earth. As per their assessment it was likely to start from Canada through parts of USA, Africa, Europe and Asia. Australia and a few islands, the poles, etc may be untouched. Every nation involved had been warned of the impending disaster. There was only one way to reduce the effect – give a push to both the moons first and then give a push to Jupiter! The push will be very minimal... a degree or two but that will be enough to divert the giant from causing serious harm to Earth. However, it will require huge amount of nuclear resources... probably all that is available in the world... but yet it can reduce the impact.

The scientific community of India under the Ministry of HRD debated the pros and cons, calculated and recalculated the data, consulted everything from folklore to the scriptures, a few reliable astrologers, data from space and the latest data from the World Space Observatory located in the outer space which was run by a joint crew from eight nations including India. They worked out the possible solution designed by Kalam. They also planned on evacuation from the impact areas. They were certain that this is going to happen soon and it is better to be prepared. This was the only chance because they knew that the vivisection of earth will give rise to floods, tsunamis, earthquakes and what not...! Chances of survival was very dim!

Those who survive,... a big question mark!

The world over had been discussing this in their respective Science Forums. The second conference of the UNGS was due shortly. Every nation had perceived the severity of the problem and their respective scientists were glued to the telescopes, computers and AI. Chile was agog with activities in all of its observatories. So were others.

The Mauna Kea Observatory, Hawai was one of the important observatories operated by the US. It had a mixture of scientists from USA and Europe. Dr. Gerald Straum the top US astronomer was scanning the entire spectrum of the Blackhole M 32. This was an enigma for him He had a cherished dream,... he wanted to go there once and dive into it! Well, he was no space traveller. He knew that probably Devyani the Angel or Stephanova or Thomson the 'Ironman' could do it. It is the job for mavericks like them. He envied them.

"It always fascinates me"

"Are those black mass in the background,... planets?" David the physicist asked.

"They appears to be forming into planets from the debris. It will take ages for them to become a proper planet" Kuntzova said. She was an expert on comets, asteroids and planets. "Leave them, man we should now be more interested in Kalam's Jupiter and Io".

Initially NASA did not give much credit to the theory propounded by Kalam. It was typical of the false pride and ego that only Europeans are the intelligent species on earth. However gradually they came to believe that it is not so. Most of the doctors, scientists, AI experts, CEOs and even few Heads of States were of Indian origin. From Pichai to Sunank to Baldev Singji of Canada to Dr. Mahadevan at NASA and so on, Indian origins dominated every field. Thew dominance of Indian brain power was beyond any doubt. This prompted the world to look up to India in any crisis. This was a time of crisis and the world decided to work together. They directed one of their satellites towards Jupiter. Kuntzova pressed a few keys and they were looking at Jupiter on the screen. Exactly then it 'shivered'!

"Oh!!" exclaimed Straum, "this guy Kalam is absolutely right."

"He is." Kuntzova said. "But how come that no one ever pursued it since '84?"

"Our big ego! We consider we are the best. Kalam and Co. are far better, they have proved it time and again. They use a combination of science, occult, astrology, scriptures, mythology and what not...everything available under the sun!"

"Yes. I had a chance to read their book called Srimad Bhagavatha. It was explained by the sanyasi of an asram. It tells all, and everything has been proved right till now. They have method of calculating time and space which they call 'Kaala'. With that, they had calculated the distances between planets, earth to Sun, to Moon and planets ages before Ptolemy or Galeleo were even born. And they were absolutely correct!" Kuntzova said. "But they died out due to the death of Sanskrit. But then... Kalaam and co are a rare variety!"

"Soon he will be addressing the UN, let us hear him".

Such debates were going on in Japan, Germany, Russia and many others. Years ago even the adventurous billionaires like Elon Musk, Branson, Adani and few others had taken interest in it. There were private underground cities already constructed with cooperation from the governments of their respective countries. Some of them had Space Shuttle service running from earth to Moon and certain other stations. Now they were also planning to colonise other planets. To avoid confusion and rivalry

UN had stepped in and all efforts of the private and governments were co-ordinated and regulated. All these had given a boost to the Space Technology since something new was being invented every now and then. The world was poised to colonise space and live in underground cities. No depression... hope... and hope! The world have been able to create a 'come what may' attitude.

The council hall at UN was cool though filled to the capacity with members, staff and some audience. The secretary General addressed them as a formality and asked India to present their plan... solution. Kalam calmly walked to the podium and placed his file and the screen controller remote on the lectern. His support staff, as usual had made rest of the arrangements. He was relaxed, casual and rougish with the dishevelled hair falling to a side. Maya had a special liking for it... "so that I can pull him by the hair". Kalam greeted the audience and said,

"We were here few weeks back and I was asked by the SG whether I have any solution... I do have one. There could be many other... we will see." He proceeded to explain the then position of Jupiter, IO and Geynemaede and other satellites of Jupiter and their probable route... as time passes the planet and its moons gets closer to the earth... The position was explained with animated video which everyone could understand. He explained the likely direction, time and distance at which Io closes in on earth. He did the same for Genymaede also. And then... "the giant passes over us at a distance closer than the one to moon! A left hook, a right thrust and a vicious uppercut"

Benjamin Levy the chief of UN's Science Department raised a hand and Kalam stopped. "I want you all to express your views of what Kalaam has shown here"

Prof Alex Barber the representative of Britain said. "We differ on the time schedule… it will take at least 50 years or more…"

There was a hum of disagreement from almost all others. Prof Lee Brandon of NASA said, "as the planet starts moving its speed may be less, but as it moves the speed will increase and the gravitational pull of Sun will be reduced. The figures projected by India is generally true" Since others were in agreement with it. Levy asked Kalam to continue.

"Now we come to the suggested solution."

Dr Athena, the Head of French Space Research Organisation said, "How about moving the earth away from the path?"

"Possible… but how much and how!?"

"Not practicable Dr Athena." said Kalam. "The reason is the two troublesome moons. We may crash into them… and then it is likely to do a reverse spin… you know what will happen then… we will have no control over anything at all. Moreover if we somehow try to move earth we may not have control over it and... there are mapped and unmapped black holes... you see!"

The conference dragged on with plans by different people and discussion on them. However, nothing seemed to be workable. The discussion was closed for the day to be continued the next day.

Kalam nursed his drink looking intently at the computer. He could not think of any other idea. Probably this must be the only idea. The phone rang, it was Maya. "I know you are in the thick of it... but still..."

"Maya, you will be surprised" he said calmly. "I have plenty of time because... this is the only plan that can work in the available time. I can have a peaceful sleep" They spoke for long. He could literally feel her near him as he fell asleep.

He had a dream in which heard someone saying,... "You never know". He woke up shivering. At first he thought that someone among his staff must have been talking. But the corridor was empty. He tried to recreate the dream but... nothing. Soon he forgot it as he got involved with the work in hand. Yet...

"YOU NEVER KNOW"!

Benjamin Levy straightened the knot of his tie and said to the mike. "Do we have some consensus... some plan?" There was nothing new. "I am happy to note that despite our small differences all of you have displayed total solidarity in saving Mother Earth. Now let us once again hear India… all yours Kalam"

"The plan that we have designed is to tackle Io and Genymaede in the first phase and in the second phase deal with Jupiter. We will push Io towards M 32 and Genymaede away from harm. They will nevertheless create some damage by way of earthquakes and cyclonic winds. In this phase the areas affected will be generally the Southwest and Northeast. Resources required are one third of all available and producible nuclear and hydrogen explosives and the' Airbenders or artificial typhoons' and Polar winds. In fact last year we tried the Airbender successfully against the asteroid which was coming from the Asteroid Belt. Judging from that effort, we feel that… Nuclear bombs and three to four Airbenders will have to be used against Io. Genymaede does not require that much effort."

The world was aware of it. It was in the month of Jan 2031 the world was alerted by Chandma observatory about a medium sized asteroid coming towards earth. India, Russia and USA together directed Airbenders which pushed the speeding asteroid away into the Kepler Belt. Had it not been done it would have smashed into the earth creating a huge crater as big or bigger, than Algeria.

The audience took time to assimilate the details. They bombarded Kalam with questions and doubts which he parried with such authority and confidence that he inspired confidence in everyone in the hall.

"Now coming to Phase 2 - the Giant! We need colossal effort to ward him off by a few degrees before it approaches our planet so that it moves away on its own accord with the push we give. As per the data and calculations,... it is possible. However there is going to be heavy damage. It will suck up huge chunks of earth... as big as... Texas, UP, Madagaskar or Peru towards it from different parts of the world!"

"Good heavens! How is it possible?"

"Dr. Barber, you are aware that the gravitational force of Jupiter is far stronger than that of earth. When it comes closer it can even pull the entire earth towards it. Because of our proposed effort and its own deviation we may escape with deep cuts all over the earth... huge gorges 10 km by 6 km in length and breadth and about a km deep. Some of it may fall back on other parts of earth obliterating whatever is there! It is the price we have to pay"

There was a pin drop silence in the hall. One of the staff wo was a good cartoonist made a quick cartoon – a huge pot- bellied figure plucking earth from here and there with hands and mouth,... it's eyes red and mouth issuing flames! The dramatic pause Kalam gave was for this... so that let the grievousness of the calamity sink in. In their minds the assembly of scientists made quick calculations... permutations and combinations...they knew that Kalam was right, there was no other way. There were many more questions, arguments and proposals.

But by the end of the day it was clear that there is only one solution… that projected by Kalaam!

"The plan is like this. D day for Jupiter passing us is somewhere around…2048. Working backwards, we place a number of space pods in this alignment (he showed it on the screen) at different distances as shown. The distance is calculated taking into account the speed at which Jupiter is moving. These will carry a number of Directional Nuclear and Hydrogen bombs/charges which will be detonated as per a pre-decided schedule. The detonation of Pod No1coupled with Directional Polar Wind (Airbender) should be able to make a two degree push to the planet. This will alter its direction of move by two degrees which will increase by the time it arrives at Pod No. 2. In similar manner the process will go on till the last one. We cannot take the risk of closing any nearer… neither do we have any more resources." He gave a pause and continued.

"We will require a total of 600-1000 bombs… that is, all the nuclear arsenal and resources of earth!"

The audience gasped in disbelief. But then, there was no other option. Kalam further explained the plan at length including the preparations that are on. The world was in general agreement to it. He further explained the division of responsibilities as proposed by the UN which would be confirmed after consulting with the Heads of States in a summit soon to be hosted by UN. During the tea break Duke, the cartoonist displayed the cartoon which was hilarious at the same time thought provoking. Someone said, "Duke, make a Gulliver like earthlyman like say… Kalam ready to fight the giant… eh?" There were many more who agreed with the suggestion. Eventually both the cartoons became celebrities!

When the conference resumed all were serious thiking of the consequences. The atmosphere was grave and ominous.

"Now comes the interesting and daring part" Kalam said with a childish grin. "I have some surprise for you"

There was a hum in the hall as everyone relaxed and became inquisitive.

"India is planning to send a manned satellite to Jupiter when it is closest to Earth. They will try to colonise it… if… they… survive!!!"

"What!!!" Entire assembly asked in disbelief.

"Yes. We are already aware that there are a number of locales on Jupiter where life might survive. So it is a wild guess and a mad plan at the face of it. But India is going ahead with it."

"Who is going to take such a risk? You can't force people like that" Barber said again.

"You will be surprised. We have too many volunteers… even from other countries including Britain. We have received a lot of queries from a large number of private enterprises from different parts of the world wanting to launch their own manned space crafts to Jupiter, sans the risk!."

Suddenly the meeting became cacophony. Every nation probably want a share of Jupiter!

Kalam had already visualised this and spoken to the UNSG for establishing a regulatory authority. Now Mr Benjamin Levy said, "please... ladies and gentlemen, calm down. We have already visualised such a schanario and have catered for it" He explained the establishing of a regulatory body which will coordinate the launching of Space Stations to Jupiter as well as controlling them on Jupiter... if they survive." The Registration procedure and recording were briefly explained. By the time the meeting concluded, the world has become one against the common threat! Moreover instead of the depressive atmosphere in which the meeting began a few months ago, today it was all excitement.

...

Back in India, in the specially created Ops Room at J Quest, Dr JJ Singh, Kalam, Kuntzova, the Space-cum Nuclear expert from Russia and Ichigava, the Outer Space expert from Japan sat in the swivelling 3D theatre like chairs looking up into the projected piece of Space. This was a planetarium created especially for Project Jupiter. It had powerful machines connecting them to all the major Space observatories, Space Stations and the Stations in

Moon and Mars. Real time data was available from all of these.

"It will require the entire Nuclear resources of the world turned into an Armada."

Dr JJ Singh spoke. "Armada it will be. Our team is already on that. Once it is ready you both will be in charge of it. Kuntzova and her team will take on Io while Ichigava and his team will take on Genymaede so that Kalam and the rest of us can take on Jupiter. Devyani and C'men will handle the landing crafts. Levy will administer the evacuation of people from the impact areas and their resettlement. Mr Graham Lundgen and Mrs Radhika Nair will handle the Coordination of the Launching and Colonisation effort by Government and private crafts. Once on Jupiter, Devyani will take over."

That was the general plan. The world had authorised India to command the operation. Kalam said, "So let us work out the details".

* * * * *

CHAPTER 6

Prithvilok.

Pritha was relaxing in the diwan. The fragrance of the flowers from the garden brought a freshness and charm. The sound of the birds added orchestra to it. Bhavani was seated on a separate single seater diwan while other helpers and maids moved around doing their cores. They were waiting for Vajrasimhan.

"I am really surprised and happy to observe the species. They are doing a wonderful job all alone" Pritha said.

"Yes, Arye. Since the first ship and that hooded being stepping out of it, they have progressed pretty fast. Now they have a number of houses and certain other Yanthra at a number of places. Is there any thapas, boons and the kind like Ravana, Bhisma and others had earlier?"

"Not at all. This time there are nothing of those because we are at the fag end of our period... Thamoguna pradhanam. Yet there had been a few brilliant ones who came and went from time to time".

"You mean, whatever they have made is all by themselves?"

"Exactly!! And that is why I appreciate them more than the earlier ones"

"Pranam Arye" The booming voice accompanied by the soldierly figure of Vajrasimhan entered the hall. Pritha acknowledged the greetings and dismissed the maids. Vajrasimhan was like a father and mentor to her.

"I mentioned something about the species, remember"

"Yes, Arye... I had also gathered some information about them from my own sources. They are doing something fantastic!"

"I want to study them in detail... it appears that they are in the know of the move of Bruha and Pushkara"

"That's news to me!"

"Me too" said Bhavani with surprise.

"I heard it from Narada. It seems that they have made some plans to ward off Bruha, Pushkara and Genemenden"

"What! The species trying to ward off Bruha...!!! impossible. Even we find it difficult and how can they do it?"

"I do not know, I want you both to find out and keep observing them more closely."

They discussed various aspects of the impending confrontation with Bruha, preparations for it and the role the species might play in it. Vajrasimhan had made thorough preparation. The plan was to first offer a weak front to Pushkara so that he comes into the killing ground and then attack him from the flank so that he is forced to extent his flank farther and farther. Indraghosha will then attack him from behind so that he come face to face with Pritha...

She wanted it that way. She will deliver him the final blow and push him into the Thamogartham. Pritha wanted to avenge Prithvas.

"I want to see his face" she said with emotion which was rare in their realm.

"You will!" said Vajrasimha. "Me and Bhavani will now have a close look at the species and report to you. Pranam arye."

J Quest Ops Room

"We expect Io to be here on............ It is likely to enter Earth's magnetic field within a week or so after that. Therefore before it enters we have to push it away towards M 32."

"That's right Kalam" Kuntzova said. "I have calculated the force required for that. We will need 12 pods each containing of ten 15 megaton DCs (directional charges). Along with it a minimum of three Ion cyclones which will continue to push it using its own velocity towards the periphery of M32. Rest will be done by M 32 itself."

"The calculations cannot be cent percent correct because..., after all... they are data. We will have to keep something in reserve for each stage" Ichigava said.

"You may take it from the resources for Jupiter since the giant will come later only" Sardarji said.

"Not a chance sir" said Kalam. "Time... time to recoup it and place it in position for the giant is not feasible"

"I feel the same way" Ichigava said and so did Kuntzova. "all the resources have to be dedicated to each of them"

"So you want to create a reserve in addition to these... right?" Sardarji asked.

"Right. The Mossad and our own RAW had been tasked to find out the existence of clandestine nuclear devices with Iran, Arabs, Africans and certain terrorist organisations. They have prepared a proper chart of the locations and quantum of those. It is TOP SECRET!" Kalam said. "We are already in touch with them"

"You have a solution for everything, man!" Kuntzova said admiring him.

"Better to be a solution than a problem... right? So now we will first make the detailed allotment and placing chart, timing and so on"

The discussion continued. It was 2032 October, the Navrathri season in India. In another two years JUICE would land in Europa and will confirm availability of water and many details about the atmosphere there.

The UN had constituted different teams for each operation. Kalam was appointed the overall Coordinator-in-Chief of all operations. There was the main team 'Project Jupiter with Kalam as its head and an assortment of scientists. Next the Io Team with Dr Kuntzova as its head tasked with preparation and execution of 'Op Io'. In similar manner Ganymede Team was established under Dr. Ichigava for 'Op Ganymede'. Then there was another organisation set up under Dr Benjamin Levy to coordinate the rescue and relief operation in the areas which were likely to be under the threat of Jupiter. The 'Gurunali' as JJ Singh called it, was going to be a series of shapeless grand canyons spread all over the world. As per the research it touched every continent and left some parts of the continents unaffected. Even the unaffected areas too may get tossed elsewhere due to the tsunamis. Since the earth was now fighting a common enemy the world has become one under the UN, sans religion, politics and nationality.

Then the 'Future Team' to coordinate the underground futuristic living headed by Dr. Sagarika Bose, another UN Deputy. All these teams had mixture of scientists, space experts, Military personnel and a variety of others from different countries.

Kalam had already announced the period of approach of Io, Genymeade and Jupiter. He also declared the dates on which Jupiter will be closest to our planet. This was for calculating the time period for launching space vehicles - manned and unmanned, to Jupiter from various governments and private agencies. The whole world was in a Jupiter hysteria! There were plenty of people who wanted to attempt colonising Jupiter. They were aware of the risks... They knew that survival possibility is very low... even if they survive, what after that... no clue... but try they must! The least time calculated for the space ships to reach Jupiter was about nine months and twenty three days. The world has become a bee hive of activities. Hundreds of Nuclear and Hydrogen pods were being readied for launch against Io, Genymade and Jupiter. A number of Space shuttles were roaming around the outer space closely observing Jupiter, Io and Ganymede. Colonies established in Moon, Outer space and on the new planet discovered, were being developed further. Few specialist space vehicles containing construction material miniaturised using nano technology were being readied for Jupiter landing.

Detailed analysis of likely area for colonisation of Jupiter was being done by Devyani and her team. The area which was presumed to have a more or less earth-like atmosphere had been identified long ago by various organisations including the Indian Space Centre. However, it was difficult to predict its position vis a vis Earth when the Giant pass through. Kalam had given the direction that all Spaceships should have extra fuel and survival material because it is possible that they may land in a different area and will have to manoeuvre to the target area. Since fuel was not a problem the space crafts carried plenty of nanoised survival items. Fuel was to be extracted from the space itself and the technology for that was widely in use. India was the only nation which had mastered the 'Light ray Speed Conversion Technology' as the world was yet to authorise its use. Because of that India had already sent a robot manned spaceship to Jupiter which had landed there in the 'Sea of Tranquillity'. The equipment in it had carried out detailed analysis of the atmosphere, soil and the ground and had confirmed that this area had a lot of similarity to Europa and had an almost Earth like atmosphere. The JUICE also was likely to provide more information. The robot ship of India, 'CHAKSHU' had sent its 'Search Drones' to investigate the entire area of the Sea of Tranquillity which was almost as big as Earth. The dates for launch, the route, etc. had already been worked out. Most of the teams were already living in the Spaceships for familiarisation. Two of them had an entire family manning it! The whole thing was utterly crazy... beyond the wildest imagination!

* * * * *

CHAPTER 7

J Quest Ops Room

"We expect Io to be here in early '44. It is likely to enter Earth's magnetic field within a week or so after that. Therefore before it enters we have to push it away towards M 32."

"That's right Kalam" Kuntzova said. "I have calculated the force required for that. We will need 12 pods each containing ten 15 megaton directional charges. Along with it a minimum of three Polar Cyclones which will continue to push it using its own velocity towards the periphery of M32. Rest will be done by M 32 itself."

"The calculations cannot be cent percent correct because..., after all... they are data. We will have to keep something in reserve for each stage" Ichigava said.

"You may take it from the resources for Jupiter since the giant will come later only" Sardarji said.

"Not a chance sir" said Kalam. "Time... time to recoup it and place it in position for the giant is not feasible"

"I feel the same way" Ichigava said and so did Kuntzova. "all the resources have to be dedicated to each of them"

"So you want to create a reserve in addition to these… right?" Sardarji asked.

"Right. The Mossad and our own RAW had been tasked to find out the existence of clandestine nuclear devices with Iran, Arabs, Africans and certain terrorist organisations. They have prepared a proper chart of the locations and quantum of those. It is of course "TOP SECRET!" Kalam said. "We are already in touch with them"

"You have a solution for everything, man!" Kuntzova said admiring him.

"Better to be a solution than a problem… right? So, now we will first make the detailed allotment and placing chart, timing and so on"

The discussion continued. It was 2032 October, the Navrathri season in India.

The UN had constituted different teams for each operation. Kalam was appointed the overall Coordinator-in-Chief of all operations. There was the main team 'Project Jupiter with Kalam as its head and an assortment of scientists. Next the Io Team with Dr Kuntzova as its head tasked with preparation and execution of 'Op Io'. In similar manner Ganymede Team was established under Dr. Ichigava for 'Op Ganymede'. Then there was another organisation set up under Dr Benjamin Levy to coordinate the rescue and relief operation in the areas which were likely to be under the threat of Jupiter. The 'Gurunali' as JJ Singh called it, was going to be a series of shapeless grand canyons spread all over the world. As per the research it left very few parts of the earth unaffected. They too may get tossed elsewhere due to the tsunamis. Since the earth was now fighting a common enemy the world has become one under the UN, sans religion, politics and nationality.

. Then the 'Future Team' to coordinate the underground futuristic living headed by Dr. Sagarika Bose, another UN Deputy. All these teams had mixture of scientists, space experts, Military personnel and a variety of others from different countries.

Kalam had already announced the period of approach of Io, Genymeade and Jupiter. He also declared the dates on which Jupiter will be closest to our planet. This was for calculating the time period for launching space vehicles - manned and unmanned, to Jupiter from various governments and private agencies. The whole world was in a Jupiter hysteria!

Prithviloka

"Unbelievable" said Bhavani.

"What is the latest Bhavani" Pritha asked. She was attired in a blue casual robe flowing from her shoulders. Her thick mane of bright golden hair hung loosely over her shoulder.

"Arye, our species are doing wonders. They have sent some Vimana in to Deerghamandala."

"What!!"...... but how do they know it?"

"Well, I don't know... From this Vimana some small chariots are now searching in all the four directions."

"Are there any humans in it?"

"No, there is a human like doll controlling it"

Pritha immediately changed her dress and asked her war council to assemble. Bhavani explained to them all that she had observed. The Vimana at Deerghamandala, small vimanas flying between Guru and Bhumi, Chandra, Mangal and other gruhas. She had also paid a visit to the ground where the species were carrying out planning to meet the threat of Guru, Pushkara, Genymendon and others. Pritha gave orders now.

"Vajrasimha, I want you to personally observe them and find out their plans. If my vision is right they are going to fight the battle for us, we just have to enhance them a bit. What is the name of that Yogi?"

"It's Kalaam... Arye!"

"Might be a part incarnation of Vishnu"

"Could be!"

Satyaloka

Narad had a smile on his lips. Lakshmi was the first to notice it. "Why do you smile, Narad?"

"This Kalki is doing a wonderful task... unlike ever before."

"What is that?" Siva asked.

"Well..., no fight, no bloodshed like in the previous yugas. He is commanding the fight of Pritha against Bruha, Pushkara and Genymendon all by the species themselves."

"Interesting" said Vishnu. "But what's he up to?"

"Oh! Prabhu, he have a viman landed in Guru griha's Deerghamandala!"

"That is really something. Does Bruha know it?"

"No, Bruha is not interested in Deerghamandala. He considers it as a cursed area"

"So are the species planning to inhabit it?"

"Likely... we will see"

"Does Pritha know about it?"

"I think so because Bhavani has been closely observing the activities of the species for some time. The other day Thejaswiny had also paid a visit to Deerghamandala."

"It is very interesting... both Pritha and Kalki are acting extremely well. But both of them will need some extra assistance from you all".

"Siva and Parvathy can help in inhabiting Deerghamandala by the species by giving their 'amsam' to selected humans... like say Hanuman or Durga" Vishnu said, "while Kalki will look after the earth"

"So be it Bhagavan" Narada said. He took leave of the trio and proceeded to watch Aditya, Bruha and Pritha.

Pritha was holding the war council. Vajrasimha had visited the species and observed them in detail and reported his findings. Bhavani also had given her findings. So did Tejaswini about Deerghamandala and the Vimana of the species. Other chiefs had explained the positioning of forces by Bruha, Pushkara and Genymendon. Indrajit who was in charge of Pushkara said.

"He is planning to hit us from the east with the main force while a diversionary force will simulate an attack from the south. I have allotted forces for both and has kept a reserve as you had asked"

Kapaleswar who was in charge of Genymendon explained his plans and Thejaswini explained her part. Pritha rose and addressed all. "Indrajit will push Pushkara to the west by expanding your forces. Pushkara will have to widen his arch which will be closer to the Thamogartha. Somdutt will tackle the diversionary attack. I will take Pushkara head on and lead him to the Thamogartham while Bhavani will release two Chakravakam from two different directions"

"Now coming to Genymendon, Kapaleswar will first block him with a small force. Then hit him hard with your main force and the Chakravakam. Bruha is initially your problem Vajrasimha."

"I have six akshouhinis placed at six locations which will needle him all the way. Once you join me my main force will give him the final thrust from the rear"

Overall… it appears to be a bold, beautiful and daring plan.

Earth

"Indeed a bold, beautiful and daring plan!" said Marshal John Sinclair, the UN Chief of Operations in his booming voice.

"Yes, provided… all nations agree." That was Akihiro the Nuclear Operation Chief.

UNSCC was on an emergency session. The SG along with Kalam and others were finalising the plans.

"In theory… they have" said Kalam. "I am sure, in practice also they will."

"They bloody well will"… murmured C'men looking at the screen in the ship. He was monitoring the UNSCC meeting.

"You men are always… men!" Devyani said laughing. "Forget them now and let us work out the lauch plans"

It was June 2040.

* * * * *

CHAPTER 8

It was just after the dispersal of the war council that Narada reached Pritha's palace. She had just disbursed the ministers and Warlords for the impending campaign and was about to retire when her Sairandri informed her of the arrival of the sage. She was overwhelmed.

"Pranam Oh great one! You have honoured me by visiting here"

"Praise be to you Devi"

She offered him a seat and had fruits and milk brought for Narada. She remained standing. Narada asked her to sit and said.

"We have been observing the activities of the Sourayootha and your tiff with Bruha... your boldness is appreciated".

"I am indeed blessed. I have decided to take on Bruha because I have a set of most faithful Chiefs and subjects. They felt that come what may we should fight our battle ourself"

"Excellent!" he smiled. "By the way, have you noticed what your species are doing?"

"Well... yes" she explained the activities of her species and how she is planning to incorporate their efforts into hers and so on. She knew that the Sage must be already aware of these and much more. "I knew that they have fared better than all of the earlier species I had in the previous Manvantharams. This time, since we have no complete incarnation I expected them to meekly submit to the Time".

"Yes... your time is almost about to finish, isn't it?"

"Hmm... it is. But then, my species had made all the difference. I never expected them to counter a menace like Bruha. He is not an earthly enemy like Ravana,, Bhishma or Duryodhana. And yet... they are taking on it admirably and not only that... colonising Deerghamandala!"

"Very impressive"

"Therefore I am now just enhancing their efforts... against Bruha as well as for Deerghamandala"

"The Trimurthy are closely watching though they will not interfere with you, Bruha and Aditya. Therefore be very careful".

"That I will be... I know Bruha well"

"May you have success in all your efforts"

Earth

Kalam was pacing the room like a wounded tiger. That was his habit and his colleagues were familiar with it.

The array of computer screens, planetarium like sky projection, a variety of other gadgets made the room look like a scene out of some sci-fi movie. His team was multinational though predominantly Indian. Devyani used to be his No 2 as she understood his mumblings and moods very well. But now she was in the spaceship; though in communication. The space displayed Jupiter and some of its moons real-time.

He looked at the globe of earth and Jupiter. CH Murthy who was controlling the jack made some movements. Jupiter started moving at a slow pace from the corner of the screen towards the opposite corner. Earth was rotating on its axis and so was Jupiter. At some point Murthy stopped and said, "this is the first impact likely"

"Greenland" said Anderson. "Probably half a day?"

"Think so" said Kalam. "May have a few earth quakes… no serious damage… move ahead, Murthy".

Both the earth and Jupiter began to move rotating. "A diagonal slash from South Canada over North America and dipping into the Pacific Ocean" the Jupiter moved and the earth rotated and it was easy to identify the impact areas… "and then parts of Russia, along Iran…to Africa to Brazil and then probably parts of Antartica" As he said the Jupiter moved and earth rotated.

"Damage assessment, Gunther" Kalam said with his pen on the pad.

"From South Canada through USA... to Russia-Mangolia-China-India-Africa-Atlantic-South America is the likely path of influence of Jupiter. It won't be a straight line... But a riffraff series of canyons and scooped up earth. The portion of the earth untouched is likely to close into the gap due to the pressure from the oceans. The oceans are likely to throw up new islands... floating lumps coming together and forming new islands... some of the present coastal regions and island may get swallowed up by sea while some might emerge out of nowhere!."

"Dr Levy has a tough task it seems. Some of these nations have enough space to accommodate their evacuees while Africa and South America will have problems"

As they contemplated and calculated the extent and depth of the likely canyons, the time schedule for evacuation, relief camps and other resources they felt that this was as good as fighting the biggest war of the world against an alien – like in the sci fi movies. They all looked at Kalam and said,

"Well, you should give a command from the Jupiter HQ that 'the evacuees will be accommodated by the nations'- you give a list... I am sure they will accept it because... at the moment, the world is looking up to one man...KALAM!"

"Thanks...... Kalam had anticipated it and had already discussed it with Levy. Valeria had already prepared the draft order.

"I will do that... Now let us tackle the giant"

They worked out every detail of the pods to be placed, the quantum of charges in each of them, the detonation schedule and of course, the launching schedule. Similar data had been prepared for Io as well as Genymaede. They had them crosschecked, confirmed and reconfirmed from all the outstations in space and Moon, Hobbes and others.

In due course six pods and four Cyclones were launched to meet Io and push in into the path of Jupiter so that by the sheer impact Io will either be thrown away or shattered into Jupiter. Another six pods and six Cyclones were launched to meet Genymaede. The 12 pods meant for Jupiter also had been launched and placed at the pre-selected points in space along its path. They were being controlled from Moon personally by Kalam.

The evacuation process began under Dr Levy. All the nations cooperated in an unprecedented manner. All the world had taken the Indian vedic adage "Loka ssamastha sukhino bhavanthu" as the universal slogan. However there were a large number of families from the 'Gurunali' areas who wanted to stay there and experience the aftermath. Despite the awareness that the chances of survival are almost nil they wanted to experience it. It was crazy... inexplicable! No one... no one in the whole world was scared... on the contrary they were all excited.

"If we survive we will be thrilled... if we perish,... well,... again we will be thrilled"!

The whole world had gone insane. However the sane ones were working overtime for the safety of the insane.

Inside the huge spacecraft named 'THRISANKU' Devyani was in command. Her crew was multinational except for her husband, Col C'men who was the 2nd-in-command also. There were eight couples including themselves. They were scientists, technicians, doctors, communicators, navigators and many such other faculties rolled into one. There were three spaceships including theirs which were officially sanctioned by the UN. All had multinational crew. GAGARIN would be launched from Russia while INCASAN to be launched from USA. THRISANKU and these two were the first ones to be launched followed by others from various countries and the private enterprises. In all there were 108 of them! Around a thousand people were going in them into the unknown with zero expectation of survival.

All these crafts were carrying a variety of equipment for making shelter, rovers, seeds, food and clothing and many such other item for an year. Since nanotechnology has been in regular use for more than a decade miniaturising was not a problem. The velocity of the crafts were going to be a problem since it was only India which had the capability of using the light spectrum. Therefore Thrisanku was expected to reach Jupiter much earlier than others.

The time schedule for the launching of the space crafts was coming closer. They were expected to cross the earth's magnetic field in 12 hours then move into their allotted orbits within another day. Thereafter, they will have to outmanoeuvre Io and Genymeade and then wait in orbit to slip into the orbit of Jupiter on a prefixed specific date and time. From the launch it would take 4 -6 months to land in Jupiter if,...... they are not destroyed by any flying objects from either of the three or pushed away to some unknown destination by the sheer force of Jupiter. Like Kalam's 'thakiya kalaam',

"Dare to dream... it will be"

* * * * *

CHAPTER 9

It was strange indeed.

From different parts of the world huge aircrafts/trains and in some cases trucks carrying nuclear and hydrogen weapon material were moving cheered by the people. Terrorism and internal as well as international rivalries had taken a backseat for the time being. The entire world was fighting a common enemy. In a month's time most of them arrived in their allotted destinations. There they were processed and reassembled into Directional Thrusting Charges (DTC). Once that was complete, they were further moved to the launching sites in USA, India, Russia, Germany, Indian Ocean and Pacific Ocean. They were loaded into the pods, calibrated and readied for the final launch.

Kalam was monitoring the launch operation from the control room in ISRO. The Io group of pods were nicknamed 'Iotas' while the ones for Genymeade were called 'Ginnies' and the ones for Jupiter, the 'Giant'. First lot to be launched was the Iotas followed by Ginnies and lastly the Giants. The Iotas were launched from USA and Pacific Ocean platforms.

"Pod 1 ready for launch... pod 2..." So it continued till the last one of Iotas confirmed readiness.

"All Iotas" Kalam said looking at his watch. It was 0440:00seconds. "Set time 0423 : 59 seconds" Even Kalam had a superstition of numbers and that is why the time was set such. Many of the Gods had eight hands!

"Done"

As the hours of the clock ticked the entire world stood still... the first assault against an alien planet... for real... was about to happen! Millions and millions of eyes were all glued to the screen in front of them in homes, shanties, pubs, hotels, palaces, aashramams, chai makanis... everywhere...the hands of the clock ticked to 0423 :45 seconds... 46...47... 48... 49... 0439... 25... 35...

"Forty, fortifive,... fifty... fiftythree... four... five... seven... fortynine...NOW!" Kalam shouted despite all his self-control.

Like a lacer fire display the ships carrying the pods rose in a brilliance of fire and then with an ear shattering sound shot out from their launching pads seeking their orbits. Kalam heaved a sigh and gulped the Chevas Regal in one go.

Similar action was followed with Ginnies also.

C'men and crew watched the fire display happening on earth from their ship somewhere in the space. "I remember the 'vaanams' of Raman the local pyrotechnician which used to have 12 steps and then burst into brilliance... nostalgia".

"Truly impressive" said Devyani. So did all others who watched it from all over the world and space, moon, and elsewhere.

The giants were to be launched after two days. The giants were differently designed and constructed as they were meant to serve as stationary transit camps in space for future communication with Jupiter (Sea of Tranquility) where the earth was intending to colonise. Each of them had docking and parking facility for space crafts. They were spaced out in a specific pattern which were expected to be repositioned after the exit of Jupiter. The farthest one-Giant 1 had already been launched from Bykanur Cosmodrome. It was the first one to be launched as it would take more time to travel into its allotted orbit and stabilise into position.

As the days passed the world looked upto India and Kalam as the saviour.

Bruhaloka

Bruha was a huge and angry person. For him power was everything. All those who were close to him including his spouse were well aware of that. Yet, he was a person of high morals too.

"Why are you so angry against Pritha when she is not at fault at all" asked Tara Devi.

"I hate her guts"

"That doesn't mean you plan to destroy her. The fault was with Pushkara who killed her husband by unfair means...!"

"I know it, but then… everyone have a soft corner for her. Aditya could've given me the chance for raising the species since I am the biggest and strongest… And Pushkara want to take revenge on the injury and insult she had done to him"

"Be warned Arya, the wrath of a woman can do serious damage… see what Droupady's wrath did to the Kauravas… my advice is to leave this yootha in peace and prosper elsewhere"

"I will certainly consider it" He noted in his mind that there is some sense in what she says… but yet… he mumbled to himself "I hate her guts"!

In the council hall all his chieftains were ready. Mahabala the Chief of Bruha's forces was ready with the final plan to be approved by Bruha. Bruha rested his huge frame on the side rest of the throne and asked Mahaaabala.

"So what are they upto?"

"Well, she is preparing to meet Pushkara first. The forces are deployed in such a pattern that the northern front appears to be weaker. Pushkara had his spies report the strength of deployment. He want to press the main strike there" Mahabala waved his hand towards the wall and a glassy screen appeared. It had the battle ground and deployment of forces displayed by symbols.

"Don't you think Pushkara will be stretching a bit?"

"No Arya. I have catered for it" said Pushkara.

"We may not be able to come to you or reinforce you since we will be busy with our getting out of Sourayootha. Though Aditya may not interfere... yet we have to be careful."

"That is no problem... I am fully prepared to handle Pritha" Pushkara appeared to be firm. Bruha liked it. "This time no foul play... direct combat" he caressed the right side of his face which was more or less branded by Pritha. His left eye turned red.

"So be it. What about Genemendon?"Bruha asked.

Mahaabala and Genemendon explained the battle plans and the preparations done for it. The caution given by Tara Devi was now thrown off because of the sheer excitement of the impending grand clash. Bruha was now excited with the euphoria of being an independent ruler. However Mahaabala was still cautious. He dismissed others and spoke alone to Bruha.

"Though Pritha has deployed her forces the way we have seen, there is something strange about it"

"Strange! What is it?"

"The deployment is not warlike but more of a supportive nature. She have kept a lot of reserve elsewhere... as if... she is not going to fight the main war!"

"How's that possible!!?" Bruha shouted. "Aditya will not interfere... Mangal and Buddh are not upto it... who else... Sani?

"Why should Sani do such a thing?" They searched for a while, cracked their brains over it but no clue emerged. At last Bruha said, "She might have made some alliance with some mercenary force of the Bahyaloka. Better to keep a watch… and have some additional reserve… Uruspathy and Jaraya"

It never struck them that the species of the planet too had a role to play… the species were insignificant in the larger affairs… for them they were just toys for fun sake.

Suryaloka

Aditya paced the vast parlour of his palace. Only Chaya Devi and two of his ministers were present. As usual he was calm and composed. Stress and tension had no place in their minds. Even when his own son Sani rebelled, he took it calmly and justified his Dharma by punishing him. Sani was carrying the three rings since then. In fact, Aditya was grooming Bruha to take over from him once the time comes. Bruha wanted to be independent… so be it… he will have to search for someone else… Sani… or even Pritha!

"Pritha is all set to fight Bruha" the queen said, "she is very bold"

"Ah! Yes. I admire her" Aditya said. "She knows that her time is up so if she colonise a part of Bruha's empire it is beneficial for her… she can easily split it off from Bruha… if!"

"I had recently visited Bruha and Pritha without their knowledge." Somadwaja the Chief of Aditya's forces said. "She is planning to allow the species to confront Bruha and enhance their effort thereby preserving her power. Very strange and very bold!"

"Indeed" said both Aditya and Chaya Devi. "In fact Narada had mentioned that her species are doing something great... but yet... can they do it?"

"It had happened earlier too. When their predecessors grew stronger and blood-thirsty, Buddha came and pacified the world for a while. Now they have again grown strong, wild, destructive, technical and scientific... at the rate they are progressing they will destroy the world sooner than Pritha's allowed time."

"But that will be controlled by her"

"Yes of course. She is now reorienting the entire destructive power of the world towards Bruha – Pushkara-Genemendon confrontation,... and she is doing it admirably well!"

"Very interesting... still, keep a watch Somadhaja" Aditya ordered his Senapathi. "Pushkara and Bruha have a grudge Against Pritha."

"Our spies have reported that Pushkara is planning a vanguard action on Pritha to throw her in Bruha's path. They want to break her gruha into pieces... she is already aware of it. She is planning to take on Pushkara in person first and later push Bruha away. She has already deployed so and have decided to leave the vanguard action to her species. She will later enhance them against all the three and later help them colonise Deerghamandala and tear it away from Bruha."

"Can she do it!"

"We will see!".

"You keep a close watch... no interference unless otherwise required"

Prithviloka

"So what is the latest?" Pritha asked the council.

"Pushkara and Genemendon has already started moving towards us. Jaraya and Uruspathy had been shifted into a special reserve. Bruha with his main forces is scheduled to move in two days."

"We are ready for them. Why have they shifted Jaraya and Uruspathy?"

"Probably to cater for any harm to Bruha's main forces... something like a rearguard."

"What about Deerghamandala?"

"It is almost abandoned by Bruha. I have already sent few of my people there without making visible presence. It appears that the species too are aiming to reach there!" Thejaswiny said.

"Excellent! But let this remain a secret with us only. As far as the forces are concerned they move according to plan. I will give the order to launch them if needed. Make many more Chakravakas... we will need them all"

"The species have launched a number of small rathas. It appears that they are launching some more vehicles also. Another interesting thing I noticed is that they have started living in underground cities in preparation for a 'Doomdsay' as they call it!"

"You mean... they are planning for the deluge...?!" All of them exclaimed at one.

"It seems so... they are aware that they will lose a large chunk of terrain in this clash"

"Wonderful! I never expected so much from them" said Pritha. "Should I pay a visit to this human Kalaam?"

"Not now Arye. That will take the initiative and spirit out of their effort. Once everything is over you may if you feel so"

"So be it... now let us go to war. Yogam!!!"

"Yogam" said all others.

Earth – 2042

Dr Levy looked at the map in front of him. It had been marked in brown and yellow. The brown were the impact areas and the yellow were the relocating sites. He had divided the entire impact area of the world into different sectors - Greenland Sector, Yankee Sector, Kosak Sector, African Sector and South American Sector each with an Officer-in-Charge for each. In most of the sectors the evacuation and relocating people were already in progress. But then there were a large number of families who wouldn't budge. Despite the Supervisors patiently explaining them the dangers of staying there, they were adamant and insisted staying on, come what may. In certain cases some private entrepreneurs have assembled space shelters which could stand the impact of being tossed up along with the chunk of land. They expected that at some stage when the movement stabilises the chunk of earth will fall on Jupiter and they will colonise that part... if survived! Others wanted to experience the adventure -perish or survive. It was beyond any explanation or logic.

Alexievich was a tall, hard muscled man. He had inherited a small piece of land from his father on which he worked hard and added many more acres. In due course he was one of the richest farmers of the commune. His children were all well- educated and had become scientists, engineers and one with the space Agency also. Though he was in the early sixties he looked no more than forty. Roughly handsome, he was adored by Misha, his wife and loved by the children. He never had to beat them but guided them well like a proper father. He was proud of his brood and proud of his achievement. Now the government says that he should relocate to camp or be ready to perish there. He called his children and discussed the matter.

Polina, his daughter who was with Space Agency explained the entire gamut of Jupiter's passage and impact areas and that they were in the impact area. This evacuation and relocation is a must unless…

Alexy had been thinking over it. He asked Misha too. She said, "Whatever decision you take I am with you"

He told the children his decision. "I have made all these and brought you up in this land. It is in my blood… I will never leave it. If I have to perish… Jupiter or whatever it will be in this land"

"But father…"

"I don't want any of you, especially you Polina to be here. We, me and your mother has decided to remain here… come what may!"

His sons and other relatives decided to relocate but Polina was adamant… "I am as stubborn as you father, we will be together… for ever!" She hugged them.

"We will dare Jupiter… if we survive, fine otherwise… I love you my boys"

Alexievich was one among many, in the Russian 'scratch' of impact area who decided to stay and experience the unknown. Others relocated with whatever they could take. Unlike the norm the Russian Government never ordered them to move, they left it to the people… for a change.

xxx

Rajat Misra was a teacher and his closest friend was Basheer Muhammad Khan. They were 'langotti yars' friends from the kindergarten level. Bothe the families were living well interacting frequently. Their children were like siblings. Khan had four children, two boys and two girls while Misra had one daughter and two sons. All children were employed except the youngest son of Mishra who was studying.

"Rajat, they want us to relocate into the camp. Ahmad says that it is true that all this area will be uprooted"

"Basheer, I have decided to stay here. I have told my wife and children that they can move if they want… rather they should because they have a life ahead of them"

"Yar, thanks that we are thinking on similar lines. But my bivi says that if I stay she too will."

"In my case all of them wanted to stay. I had to convince them with difficulty that they should move and live on but Uma doesn't. She is adamant and so is Rahul."

"Same here too, Meher says she will stay with us"

They were one of many such families from India. There were people from Sikkim, Bihar,,MP, Gujarat, Rajasthan and some from Karnataka. Some of them had relocated to the impact area just to experience the unknown. Four of the big business houses of the country had prepared a landing craft as per the designs given by ISRO. They thought that no one would volunteer for such a risky mission. However when they advertised they were in for a surprise. There were qualified pilots, doctors, engineers, various skilled personnel, students applying for the jobs. Pay was not a concern, the thrill was. In fact it was a problem of plenty! The result was that they could assemble a group of excellent crew.

Since the people unwilling to relocate were many, the governments of the respective countries finally left it to themselves. In some cases it was the parents who had decided to remain while in others it was the younger generation. In certain cases whole families were staying. It brought in a new love and affection within the families as well as a sense of never before comradery between total strangers. There were no tension... only a sense of de je vu!

Kalam had foreseen such a situation and designed gadgets, igloos and many other "survival kit" for the people who wanted to stay. It was a surprise for them when the respective governments provided them such kits free of coast. Even the companies which were producing them took only the construction charges. One of the MDs of such company, Tehmina Tata said,

"Our organisation had generated plenty of profit and resources. At this time we need no profit... just nominal" It was echoed by TESLA, ALIBABAS, MUSK and many others.

In the temples of India, there were special yaagam and archana (certain vedic rituals of worship) in the name of Guru/Brihaspathi, the deity of one of the planets of the

Indian zodiac) as well as Bhoomi were being conducted. Specific manthras(hymns) were being chanted by masses organised by certain Achaaryas were also being held. Even people from other religions participated in the chanting. They believed that because of that Brihaspathi will be pleased and Bhoomidevi will be enhanced... Such rituals were being conducted world over in the Indian temples located in other countries, Churches, Mosques and other religious institution s all over the world.

Well! The world was ready for Jupiter!

* * * * *

CHAPTER 10

ISRO

It was happening...!

Io had begun to move into an orbit dangerously close to earth. Still it was not visible to the naked eye. Ganymede too was tracked. Hubble was constantly in touch with Kalaam and so were all the other observatories deployed in the space. The Moon Station sent photos of all the three. It made the calculation and assessment of move of the planet and its satellites easy.

The first impact was hot winds...in the Arctic polar cap as Io approached earth. It caused some melting of snow...the water gushed out into the Arctic ocean but subsided after two days without much damage. Certain countries like Tavalu and other islands which were already sinking were swallowed up by the waters. However the UN had already seen it long ago and had the people relocated to other areas. Neverthless, the ice continued to melt slowly but steadily causing floods in certain areas of Greenland and norther Russia. However it was moving in the expected manner and hence there were no major damage.

As the Iotas started firing in their sequence Io started moving away like a circular kite in the wind. As the fourth Iota was fired Io moved farther...

Prithvilok

"Arye, Pushkara has deployed his forces for attack" Vajrasimhan said looking at the crystal plate in front of him.

"Good, let Dandayodha confront Pushkara... he should make Pushkara extend to the west as per plan... right" She already had the reports that the species are pushing Pushkara towards the Thamogartha... a strange coincide! She will just enhance the effort of the species... Pritha had a thrill... to day she is going to teach a lesson to Pushkara which neither Pushkara nor Bruha will ever forget. She watched the crystal plate and followed every moment of the battle. Pushkara had expected resistance but not Dandayudha for he was one with magical powers. But Pushkara was not worried. He ordered his troops to outflank him to the west. He had catered a reserve to charge from the east and thereby cut off Dandayudha. But his reserve under Gurukripa was being held by another force of Pritha commanded by Swathaswetha. Swathaswetha was gaining on Gurukripa. Pushkara had to do something. He asked Gurukripa to withdraw and join him. Gurukripa advanced from the south while Dandayudha was pushing in from the East. The south and west were still free to go. He immediately altered his direction of strike... he was too confident... suddenly there was a series of jerks... he was aghast... he didn't know what hit him... he had to do something... because... he found that he was getting into the path of Bruha!

Bruha was watching the battle as well as steering his gruha out of the Suryaloka. Genymendon had already inflicted some damage on Pritha. He was happy... now Pushkara will cut her into pieces and he himself will scatter her gruha into bits as he goes by. It was then Mahabala shouted,

"What the hell is Pushkara doing! He seems to be pushed by some force..."

"What force? Who could it be... not any from our Yootha..." Bruha said.

"Has Pritha managed any help from outside our Yootha... any mercenary force" Mahabala asked Asitha, his Chaara Sachiv.

"No Sir... none"

"Nor will Aditya permit it... I know him... but then who?"

"Z... He is coming to our path!!"

"C'mon... ask him to move away... we can't stop now" Bruha was aghast. What has Pritha got in defence? Any secret weapon? An ally? None of his spies had reported any such movements at all. He heard Mahabala talking to Pushkara. Pushkara appeared to be confident and he was moving out of the path. Bruha slowed down as he wanted to see how Pushkara is giving the blow to Pritha. He never liked her for her guts but yet admired her courage... as a warrior to warrior.

However they forgot that the species too had a role to play to protect their planet!

Pritha observed Pushkara moving slightly to the west to allow Bruha safe passage. This was her moment... now Bruha will be away and Pushkara is all alone. She knew that Bruha will not come back to save Pushkara because it will slow him down. She shouted with full vigour...

"YOGAM!!!" Her forces under her personal command moved like an inverted half- moon... ! Pushkara saw them coming and ordered his troops to form a Thrisool with he himself leading the centre. Pritha's forces clashed with Pushkara's Thrisool and they easily dissected both the sides. Pritha ordered Bhavani to launch the Chakravaakam on them both. As the unexpected cyclone like wind enveloped them, both flanks of Pushkara were blinded. Some of them were already too close to the Thamogartham.

Pritha drew her husband's sword which had special powers and shouted "Now!!!" Her forces fell on Pushkara along with three special Cahakravaakams. Pushkara tried the only thing he could do... to outflank them and hit from the back. As he began the outflanking manoeuvre suddenly a reserve force of Pritha rushed them. He had no way but to move aside... There was some sudden big shove... his Mukhya Senapathi shouted in alarm... Aarya Pushkara... we are being tossed... into the Thamogartham. Even Pushkara could feel the shock... What was it...!

Bruhaloka

"What the hell is Pushkara upto?!!" shouted Bruha.

"He is in the path of the Thamogartham... Pritha has somehow managed to push him... and still pushing... shall we..."

"We can't stop and go back now... Pritha the devil! Pushkara... I am sorry...I have failed..."

Pushkara's face was a mask of terror, he didn't allow Bruha to complete but said, "No Bhagavan... I have failed you... I am sorry!"

...

"What is Genemendon upto!!!... he too is coming in our path!" Bruha was angry and perturbed.

"He appears to be pushed towards us by Pritha and... something else" Mahabala said. He asked Genemendon, "Gyan why are you now moving into us?"

"Senaadhyaksh, I am being pushed by some invisible forces... Pritha has some help from somewhere... in addition Bhavani has conjured up a new weapon... Chakravakam... I had nothing to defend"

"Any way, you have done what you were tasked to, now try to move away from our path and follow us"

"I will, Mahabala"

Prithvilok

Pritha was now face to face with Pushkara. He was being pulled into the Thamogartha... his face was full of mortal fear and fury... Pritha delivered the final blow which shook his chariot and pushed it with full force of the Chakravaka towards the Thamogartha. She asked the charioteer to stop and watched Pushkara and his forces being swallowed up into the Thamogartha.

Pritha could see Pushkara's face... it was a mask of fury, surprise and fear. He tried to steady but suddenly there were some sudden shivers! His forces were being shaken by some sudden successive shock waves! Pritha knew it to be that of her species. She waited... Pushkara was now trying to manoeuvre his forces away from the Thamogartha... She signalled Bhavani. When the Chakravaka hit them Pushkara could not see anything... his forces were piling up on each other... as no one could see anything they just drifted in the direction of the pressure...

"Hmmmm...!!!" Pushkara heard the deep hum... he knew it... he shouted at his force "STOoooooo...P!!"... they could hardly hold, the shudder and the wind was chaotic... when the clouds and dust cleared, he knew that the game was up... the pull of the Thamogartham was beyond his control now.

Pritha looked him in the eye and said, "Go Pushkara, nothing will save you now, not even Bruha!"

"You...!!"his face a mask of fury and fear.

Pritha watched triumphantly as Pushkara and his forces being swallowed by the whirlwind of Thamogartha. She felt a peculiar kind of elation. She mumbled to herself, "Yes my love... I have avenged you finally!"

For a while she stood alone... then controlling herself she heaved a sigh of relief... 'now I am ready' she told herself.

"Arye Genemendon had inflicted some minor damage... but..."

"What!!"

"Our species have pushed him away... into the path of Bruha"

"Excellent! I am so proud of my species... now let us tackle Bruha"

Pritha, Indrasena and all her other deputies were jubilant. Since Pushkara and Genemendon was out of the way Bruha was the only scare now. She knew that Bruha is more interested in going away from the Yootha than attacking her or Mangal. However, he will inflict some damage... he had charged Pushkara with it, now that he was out of the way, Pritha knew that she can handle the damage Bruha may cause to her. Instead of wasting effort to stop it she decided to let it happen... just control it. Her Senaadhyaksh immediately ordered the forces into that mode so that damage suffered will be minimal.

"What is the news from Thejaswiny?"

"She has already sent a small force to Deerghamandala to make it habitable for the species. She has reported some Vimana sort of things moving in the direction of Deerghamandala from Prithvi"

"Oh! Vishnu! Great work! We will soon occupy it once Bruha proceeds out of the Yootha, and gradually break it away from him… in any case he considers it as a cursed area… good for us… get on with the plan"

THRISHANKU

They had already moved into the orbit of Jupiter. It will be closest to the Earth in another two to three months. It is then that all the spaceships will finally get into the orbit. Thereafter, it is just luck!… if survived they may be able to land in Jupiter in about six months' time. Once they enter the Jupiter orbit the robot will take over and all the human crew will go to deep sleep in self- contained capsules. The robot was named 'Quixot' after the famous character.

"Dr. Kalaam, it was a great show!" Devyani said into the screen. Most of her crew were present there except those who were on watch. C'men waved at Kalaam.

"Thanks…why so formal? Tell me one thing, did you observe any other magnetic force or some such thing, close to Io or Genymede?"

"Yah!" C'men said, "we tried to analyse it… find a location… but… nothing"

"It appears to be some sort of galactic cyclone." said Boer, the astro-scientist... But strangely a directional one... never heard of... we couldn't risk getting closer"

"It is ok... it has helped us in some way" Ichigava said. "we are trying to track it... but it has disappeared somewhere without a trace... very strange!"

"You are now close to deep sleep..." Kalam had a sense of agony but he quickly concealed it. Devyani could understand it. She put him into the right spirit.

"The Giant is awe inspiring! To think that in a few months' time, we will be having breakfast there... thrilling man, absolutely mindboggling!"

"True! All others are in the orbit now...except one from China... some malfunction... crashed into Genymede"

"We saw it and have recovered two capsules... they are safe and under medical care"

"Great news! No wonder they call you Angel... I will give it to the press".

The papers, channels and all the social media were agog with the news of Io and Genymede being pushed away. They had the videos of Io moving towards the blackhole obtained from Hubble and certain other orbiting observatories. World over the temples, churches, mosques and all other places of worship were holding special prayers and offerings, bhajans, homam and such other rituals for the wellbeing of Earth and its defence against Jupiter. The sensational rescue operation by 'Angel' of the two capsules from the crashed Chinese Spacecraft too was big news.

China awarded Devyani with their highest award, The Medal Of The Republic!

Earth 2044

Once Io and Genymede out of the way the world heaved a sigh of relief. In the meanwhile, the effect of these two moons on earth were being assessed real-time. The melting of ice from the pole was still continuing and was flooding the seas. Certain islands which were expected to be lost were swallowed up by the sea. There were miner volcanic activity under the Pacific Ocean and Atlantic Ocean. Four new Islands had risen from the oceans and were still rising slowly.

The world was now gearing up for the **'Jupiter Impact'**. In fact, it had begun years ago. The erratic climate changes, untimely rains, winds, landslides and cloudbursts had already put the world in a fizzy. Till Kalaam explained the 'Jupiter Impact' people believed that these were due to environmental degradation caused by the development activities. Scientists could not explain the behavioural transformation taking place in humans, animals and even on vegetation. Humans had loss of sexual appetite, psychological disorders, increase in violence and such other emotional transformations... Now they knew that it was basically the 'Jupiter Impact' and were finding cure for them. Most of the world relied not on allopathy... but on the oriental systems of medicine, Ayurveda, Chinese Therapies, Japanese Therapies Yoga and meditation. Largely world began to follow a satwik living. The animals were generally quiet, uneasy and occasionally growling as if they were having some premonition. So were the birds, they were not quiet, on the contrary, they were making more sounds. There were strange behaviours in the sea animals, fish and insects. Mosquitos had vanished and a few other such insects too. The atmosphere was getting warmer and foggier.

'IT'... was coming...!!

Dr Levy looked at the screen. It was more like the earth spread like a flat sheet of paper, he along with two of his assistants were in an air car capsule was hovering over it. It was specially designed by TATAs. All the physical changes that had occurred since the beginning of move of Jupiter had been recorded real time over it. The disappeared Islands, the new ones, earthquakes, tsunami, et al was there. The impact areas were marked in red and had been given different names. His console had the communication set up with each of the eight Zonal Commanders.

All the impact zones have been evacuated except for those adamant families who insisted to stay and experience it. The underground cities were working for some time now. Most of the major powers were working from the underground offices.

Jupiter was closing now.

In 'Thrisanku' the crew checked one final time all the controls and machines. C'men addressed them. "So, now we go to sleep for a few months. Doc has already administered the sustainer-cum-retainer... we wake up on a bright day in Jupiter!"

He solemnly put each of them in the pods and gave a hug and reassuring smile. He turned to the Commander Devyani and said. "All set Commander! Now only you and me are left. Quixot will take over in another ten minutes."

"Yes" she spoke on the mic to Kalam "we are ready... going to sleep...will speak to you from Jupiter!" She switched the mic off and walked to her pod. C'men stood looking into her eyes and said, "I want you to know that you are the best woman I ever met, have and will ever...I love you so much...' he kissed her. She pulled his arms around him as if inhaling every atom of his body into herself. "Chandru, let's have our brood of children in Jupiter" Without another word she entered her pod, her eyes were full; and C'men closed the pod. He had one last look around and spoke to Kalaam.

"Kalaam, bye now, will speak to you from Jupiter" He switched on the closing button of his pod. It was 15th August, 2044 -97th Independent Day of India!

At 2359 hours Quixote said in the mic. "All pods asleep, monitoring. I have taken over"

On ground, Kalaam took a deep breath and shifted his eyes from others. He had tears welled up in it. Still controlling himself he said "SUBHYATHRA"

Thrisanku moved into the Jupiter's orbit. It will keep going along with Jupiter for a while and enter into its magnetic field and follow the orbit towards Sea Of Tranquility. There... one day... they will create NEW EARTH!!!

Similar action were being done in the 150 plus other ships too. All of them had been given different orbits and had been launched at different timings so that they do not clutter up or create accidents. If they survive, they will all land on Jupiter in an area of 84 earth sq km. Rest will be decided after the survivors contact each other.

Brahmloka

"This human lady Devyani is perhaps a reincarnation of Durga" Narada said.

"What makes you think so Maharshi, I haven't taken any incarnation since Threthayugam"

"Arye, she had rescued people from one of their vimaana like contraptions that had been destroyed by Genymendon!"

"She is really something, it seems"

"Which she is. They are planning to occupy Deerghamandala of Gurugriha and Pritha has sent Thejaswiny to make it more habitable for the species"

"It appears that Pritha and her species have outwitted Bruha and Aditya. They might tear away Deerghamandala from Gurugriha and set up a colony of species there and gradually build up on it from Prithvi" Siva said.

"So Aditya is likely to have two sets of species soon... interesting" Brhamavu said with a smile.

They further discussed Bruha, Mangal and other worlds.

Prithaloka

Thejaswini watched the activities of the species. The vimanas were flying towards Bruha. Bruha haven't noticed or bothered as they were just like few pebbles floating around. She informed Pritha and she asked her to gently guide them without their knowledge towards Deerghamandala. Her forces had already occupied the area and were gradually making it suitable for the species to live as Pritha had directed...

"Just give them an atmosphere... nothing more... let them create their own and flourish. You will remain there only, as the Gruhapathy".

Bruhaloka

Bruha viewed the way ahead. He had to get out of the Sourayootha and then proceed towards his target which was many yojanas away from there and relatively safe and stable area. There were no other grahas or yoothas close by to disturb him. However now first, he has to get out.

But before that he wanted to give a big blow to Pritha. His shaasthrajna sangh had prepared the special sasthras he had ordered. His plan was to carve a piece of her Gruha so that it will gradually break into pieces. He had formed a huge curtain between him and Aditya by his 40 odd sena vibhag. Still he had more than 30 vibhags with him. Only Pushkara has been lost. Genymendon has joined him. Bruha had detailed three vibhag to inflict the damage on Pritha's gruha. The carved up portions will be dumped in Deerghamandala and once he stabilises, he will cut it off and dump it in the Thamogartham, so that his curse will be gone for ever.

Bruha now turned his attention to the advance.

Earth

Now it was happening!

Jupiter could be observed even without any telescope in the northern sky. It was bigger than the moon and multi-coloured but not very bright. Report of siting had started pouring in from many parts of the world.

"Majestic"!

"Scary!!!"

"Amazing... a hundred times bigger than the moon!!"

"What's that colour patches... are they gas?"

"Is it where our people are trying to land!... hope they do"

And many more.

The world over there was an excitement. The news of confrontation with Io and Genymede and their subsequent diversion had given a big boost to the morale of the world. Now Kalaam had become a near incarnation for many.

However for Kalaam and Levy there was no excitement but total concentration. They have taken all the precautions... yet! There are always the imponderables and unseen contingencies.

The first land mass to be pulled up was of Greenland. The animals knew it earlier probably. The wild life wardens of Northeast National Park observed strange behaviour of the Polar Bears and Walruses. They were still... as if looking for something. Since the human population was almost zero except for a few officials and scientists who had already been moved to safety there was nothing much to worry. But for those who observed the action... it was scary... unbelievable! A report said,

'At first there was something similar to a typhoon, but very extended variety... began swirling... for almost the whole day... then dust and blocks of earth began jumping... two days after that, all of a sudden a huge mass of earth the size of Iceland rose like a stone from a catapult... for several hours nothing could be seen or heard... dust and darkness... noise of water seething... it was six hours since... there was a woosh and an earthshaking TTHHUUMMPP...roar of water could be heard. It took a day for the dust to reduce. Through the curtain of dust it could be seen. Apart of the land mass that went up had fallen back in a huge heap... a new mountain covered by water... there were other mounds also some floating... some like islands...!!'

Levy read the report and heaved a sigh, he spoke to Kalaam. "First strike as expected... damage assessment will follow. No loss of life to humans but animals,... could be. A new mountain and small isles have come up... the ocean have entered into Greenland..." He was now contemplating the damage the Giant is going to cause. It was June 2044.

The Giant pods were charged and ready to be fired as early as June 2044. The first five of them were fired in September as Jupiter entered the danger area of earth. The cyclones also were fired at the Giant. The sudden impact was relatively small but it did produce the desired effect. It enhanced the already wavy planet to waver further by a degree plus. Jupiter diverted slightly away from its path... veered away from a direct crash on part of earth. Had it not been successful earth would not have been able to take the impact... it would have been crushed like a lemon under the tyre of a car! Now it will pass the earth in very close... dangerous vicinity.

It will be few months before they fire the other pods. In the meantime Jupiter was going to cause lots of damage. The world and earth were ready to bear it as it was unavoidable.

Earth: January 2045

Kalaam looked at the screen… only dust and smoke and water… it was raining heavily. He could see islands floating with parts of their townships of industries or whatever they had still on it. He focussed on to the houses… most of them were locked… in some of the areas he could find people moving around helping each other to channelize the flooding waters, save the people and animals from the flood…! His eyes welled up.

"Maya! Just look at the people… no desolation, anguish. They are so happy to undergo the suffering"

"They believe in God… in you"

"I am just another human…"

"But now for the world, you are God… we all believe in you, don't ask me how"

Yes, the entire world believed in him sans religion, nationality, gender or anything. His predictions had come true. The disaster was almost on the same lines that he had predicted. They had witnessed unbelievably Io being pushed into the Blackhole, Genymede being redirected onto Jupiter and the defensive measures against Jupiter. All these reinforced their faith in him and India.

"The pods are ready for firing" the mic crackled. He looked at the screen as Akito focussed it on to Jupiter. "The Giant is now approaching the target area… probably tomorrow morning it will be in line"Akito said.

"I feel that we may have to re-time the pods... see this report from CHANG'E 4"

Akito studied the report from the Chinese Moon Station and was intrigued. How can the artificial cyclones be so strong that it could push Jupiter more than what they had calculated. Even though the scientists world over put together had created these cyclones combined with polar winds were powerful,... but against a planet... that too of the size of Jupiter, its power was very limited. Therefore they had expected that the pods and cyclones together would be able to give deviation of about one degree plus at the most. That was enough to set the Giant onto a path which was less harmful to Earth. But this... unbelievable...

... TWO AND A HALF DEGREES!!!

It would be a big relief for earth as well as for the space crafts launched to land in Jupiter. If it is true, the pods will have to be re-timed. They cannot remain in orbit longer... already two of them had been crashed by some meteor splinter from... may be Calisto or Europa since Jupiter does not emit any such splinters. He did a quick review of the deviation with Kalaam.

"I can't believe it Kalaam"

"Neither me... but there is no time to do a detailed analysis though we will put GAGARIN on it. Let us rework the pods"

He had already asked GAGARIN, the Russian Space Observatory in space as well as CHANG'E to analyse the data in detail so that earth can utilise it for further operations. In the meantime they retimed the pods.

* * * * *

CHAPTER 11

They saw it...!

From the Southern shores of Hudson Bay the ground started swelling up...almost touching the outskirts of Ottawa... Minneapolis... Kansas City... Omaha...Denver... Phoenix... it was generally in this direction, a jagged line... touching Oakland in the North and Oklahoma in the south...dipping into the Pacific Ocean. For days it swelled up in hillocks and massive lumps... and suddenly on the third day it lifted slowly...

Kalaam remembered reading in one of the Indian epic about the time when mountains used to fly! The legend of Mainaakam ! The swelled up earth rose dropping debris, trees and dust... gathered speed and went up and up faster... as if propelled by some invisible giant rocket! As it progressed the huge lump began to freeze and soon it was out of sight for naked eye. An Indian and a Russian spaceship reported it moving towards Jupiter at increased speed. It left a huge canyon to which seas and rivers were flooding in. The spaceships could not trace the families who stayed in those areas... though they hoped to hear some signal from them... Kalaam and Levy had special communication equipment designed for them and taught them how to use it. If they survive..., the earth will wait for a signal... for ever!

Kalaam and Levy were aware that the next lot will be more serious than this one since the magnetic field of Jupiter will become more intense in a few days and then as it is diverted, it will reduce... IF...!

Damage assessment as well as surveying the canyon was in progress by the teams- in-charge of those regions. Ashley Cooper was hovering over the entire area in his module surveying the damage. He could see some carcasses floating... humans and animals. "It is like a combined strike by cyclone, storm, landslide, volcano eruption and what you have... one volcano is new... visible... generally looks like a deluge!' His teams continued search in different directions.

February 2045

The night after the first strike, Russia reported earthquake in its North-eastern region... beyond measurable scale! The intensity was beyond extreme. However since population there was sparse and had been evacuated, it was the terrain that suffered the damage. The terrain split into too many canyons allowing water from the East Siberian and Latvian seas to gush into them. The pieces of land mass soon became floating islands.

Further southwest, parts of Lower Russia and Northern region of Khazakisthan bulged up into a mountainous shape and began to shiver... Buildings and structures collapsing...fire and thunder like roar... then, suddenly as if plucked out by some force the huge mountain rose... moved in a southwest direction... parts of it fell all over Turkey, Syria, Jordan and Saudi Arabia after a day. Other part was sucked into the orbit of Jupiter as reported by various observatories.

At the same time parts of Mangolia, China and India was also being ravaged. North West Mangolia experienced huge tremors, earthquakes and landslides... the land did not rise but shifted. However in China it was a different story. The Sinkiang region was almost pulled out in one go along with parts of India- Punjab and Rajasthan and some parts of Punjab of Pakisthan. It was unbelievable! Some of the mountain regions withstood the pull while plains and other areas succumbed and vanished into the Giant... some fell back into the Ocean.

Africa suffered worst... It was literally scooped up along the centre... from east to south west. The upper edge of the canyon bordered Sudan to Nigeria while the lower edge, along Somalia to Angola! The entire land mass moved as one continent and shot out towards the Giant. The canyon was filled by water both from Indian Ocean and Atlantic Ocean. Those who have been evacuated watched the horrible sight on TV. Many of them went into sudden depression, few died of shock. The satellites reported Africa forming into two new land masses and floating away from each other.

Many of the islands had either submerged in the sea or had floated away in different direction; new landmasses had come up at a number of places some joining with existing islands some just floating away in some or other direction. The nature was uncontrollable... it was redesigning the earth.

In South America it culled away huge blocks from the central to lower portion of Brazil, Urugay and Paraguay. Thereafter, the Giant left a long gash in the centre of Argentina and Chile before it entered the sea. The waters of the oceans redesigned the South American continent. There were Tsunamis in the South Pacific and Indian Oceans. The Antartica did not suffer much damage except some mild quakes and cracks on the surface.

As the re-timed pods and the cyclones were fired the Giant was safely pushed away from the Earth's periphery. Jupiter continued its journey. In the meanwhile, the space ships including 'Thrisanku' were progressing irratically towards Jupiter. Robots were controlling the ships except a few. Even they, later handed it over to robots as the fatigue and heaviness was too much for the human body to bear. By end of Jan 2045 all ships were being steered by robots. By then they had moved into the orbit of Jupiter since that was the closest Jupiter was to Earth. Two ships were reported missing, probably dived into Europa or Calisto or may be crashed onto some debris. Yet all the observatories on earth as well as in space and Moon were on the listening watch... some signal... from somewhere... hoping... and hoping!

Prithaloka &Bruhaloka

"Give them a helping hand Bhavani" Pritha said. Bhavani directed her forces and several chakravaakam which forced Bruha to alter his path.

"Whatt's it!" Bruha shouted as he felt the sudden force affecting his troops.

"Appears to be some strong Chakravaakam and some explosion... I am reorganising the troops" Mahabala was already in communication with Kailasothaman who was facing Pritha's forces.

"Is anyone helping her?" Bruha roared.

"I don't think so... none from this yootha or any other. But..."

"What?"

"Kethumaalan reported that the species of Pritha are doing something"

"Ha ha...!"Bruha laughed. "When the entire yootha can't stop me, you think the species can?"

"But they can disturb us"

"If so," Bruha paused for a moment... "CRUSH THEM TOO"

Though Bruha had to divert a bit he had already tasked two of his Chieftains to deal deadly blows on Pritha. 'Cut it into bits and pieces... scatter them'. Both the chieftains launched their forces with that purpose in mind. But neither they nor Mahabala or Bruha had a clue about what Pritha had planned. She had expected something of the sort from the reports of the deployment of Bruha. She knew that she cannot shield the brutal and heavy force of Bruha but had catered to counter it so that the damage would be minimal. In addition, she had the species! They had even created some sort of powerful cyclone which multiplies its power by each rotation. In fact, those could have made a very insignificant effect on the Gruha, though they were enough to counter the bi-pointed thrust of his chieftains. Bhavani augmented the cyclones created by the species. The result was such that not only Kailasotthama and Yuradheeswara,even Bruha felt the impact. Pritha saw the damage being done to her Gruha. She saw the terrain being scooped up, being pulled towards the Deerghamandala and some being scattered. She instructede Thejaswiny to concentrate on all that was coming towards Deerghamandala.

"I want them to stick to Deerghamandala intact. Give an atmosphere so that the species which are in it survive... to create a home there"

"It will be done Arye"

Bruhaloka

Bruha moved to his Vichar Kaksha with his ministers and informers. Taara Devi too was present.

Bhanudeva the Planning –in-Chief opened the vision on the open space. It was more like a vast movie screen...

a part of the Cosmic Universe where he was taking them. Still, it was far away. It might take another half century or more (in earthly terms) to reach there. He said,

"Maharaj, you see the open space north of Chathur Yootha. It is the safest and most suitable location for us. It is away from Sourayootha and other yoothas. We will be independent."

"Good, take us there as planned. Hope all of our group are together"

"Except for Pushkara. Genymendon have suffered some damage but not very serious"

"What about the Prithvi... she got her lesson, I think"

"Far from it!" Tara Devi spoke. "Her gruha is intact except for lot of gashes we, Genemendon and others inflicted. It will heal in time. She had her revenge on Pushkara... manoeuvred beautifully and sent him to the Thamogartham! She even smashed Genymendon onto us! I learn that she and her species have worked together... a first anywhere."

"Devi, we have taken two vimanam like vehicle of the species... they are with Uradheeswara"

"That's good" said Taara Devi. "Do not destroy them but nurture them... they could be our new species... what do you say Aryaputhr?"

"I think she is right... whatever is gone is gone... let us begin afresh." Bruha ordered. He further told Mahabala to cut off Deerghamandala with the scooped up portions of Prithvi as they cross the Thamogartham. "The cursed piece should wander here and there before getting swallowed by the Thamogartham."

Bruha and his team was so sure that nothing can change it. They never tried to analyse Pritha's mind and preclude it's consequences. Only Thara Devi had apprehensions but they were ignored by the warlords and Bruha since he felt that he was too big to be disturbed by someone as small as Pritha. Well... Pritha had different ideas for it; Deergha mandala was going to be...

Her new Prithvi!

Thrisanku

It was early March 2045. The orbit of Jupiter was too big but Kalam and his team had planned the space ships to go along the orbit for a while and then divert into Jupiter. The Sea Of Tranquility was the target since research had shown that this area had an atmosphere. Against the Giant the array of ships looked like mosquitos around a mega sized flying balloon. The robots moved them into the orbit to go along Jupiter. They went along the Giant for two months at speeds matching to the Giants rotation. It was early part of June that J QUEST felt that it is time to take the plunge. Most of the crafts were not even visible though there were occasional blips coming on the screen from them. Earth was on the blind side to the Giant, often. Once the decision was taken it was communicated to the ships.

The robots adjusted the navigational meters and awaited the time signal. However due to the unexpected change in the deviation of Jupiter the earlier calculations has to be changed. Some of the ships had already moved into orbit as they found that they are closer to Jupiter than others. There was no time for course correction as communication was erratic. Earth had already given them the time signal on 18 June 2045, 1847hrs. The robots fired the booster engines and the ships slowly changed the direction. After a pre-determined pause of four hours and 23 seconds they fired the main booster which propelled the ships into the direction of Sea of Tranquility. Two ships which were already into the orbit were on their own. Now, it will be another two months or more for the ships to approach the landing area... if... they had survived. It was a painful wait for all the monitoring stations all over the world on ground, in space and in Moon.

They waited with abated breath...!

* * * * *

CHAPTER 12

His father was a Budoin. He himself had many traits of his father, the rough exterior and a warm interior. Tall with a thick moustache, Hanif was a figure anyone would like to be friendly with. But today he was in no friendly mood to the city police who had come with the instructions to relocate him and family with many others since the area was in the danger zone. Hanif told them in no uncertain terms that he and family will stay there, come what may.

"It's none of your fault Inspector."

"Your children have a future... you want to block it? We have no idea what will happen here"

He hesitated a moment and looked at the family. Aisha said, "The children will go with you Inspector, but I and my husband will remain here" Hanif didn't say a word, in his mind he said 'so be it'

...

There were many like him from different countries who refused to budge. In some cases it was the whole family with children and livestock, whereas in some it was only the husband and wife with one child or so. Since the UNO had insisted that the final decision should be left to the individuals, there was no compulsion, only persuasion.

The first land mass that was sucked into Jupiter had no human beings. But some livestock and pets were still there. Strangely the animals stayed silent. As the land mass rose and started freezing the birds and animals burrowed into the earth, into the foliage and wherever they can and closed their eyes. Months later it was only a few which could open their eyes! Then the other landmasses which had human population began to rise up.

...

It was dark and all foggy. A typhoon type of wind was howling its way through the trees. Harjinder Singh and family consisting of his wife Jasbir Kaur, son Kulwanth Singh, a sturdy tall nineteen year old and two daughters, Manpreet and Thanpreet had decided to experience it. The children were more excited than the parents. Their immediate neighbour a family from Kerala had exchanged their daughter with Harjinder. So Manprit stayed with Mukundan Menon while his daughter Nalini went with Harjinder. Menon and family with Manprit moved to the evacuation camp while Singh stayed on. Harjinder told his son to close all the doors and open only the small windows. They felt the area undergoing a small earthquake. However in a few hours something else started happening. Kulwanth announced,

"Papaji...we are moving...up" Both Thanpreet and Nalini were glued to the windows "Its magnificent bhayya..." a sudden gust of wind made them close their eyes... Cold winds... as if putting ice over the whole area. They had catered for capsules of oxygen which could last them for over two to three months. Harjinder moved them into the special capsule home designed for such families by Kalaam and Elija, an Alaskan scientist. It was more of a container with beds, washrooms, kitchen all telescoped. They had nanoised food supplies to last for four months in addition to normal food items. Soon they could only hear a continuous 'Woosh'. They were feeling dizzy and gradually slept wherever they were. All around darkness spread.

...

Iraq and Iran felt devastative earthquakes, cyclone and some eruption. Oil erupted from the wells as high as Eifel Tower and wooshed out in a flaming spiral. The Northern and Southern parts of Africa remained generally unaffected. Levy had moved most of the people from the affected areas into North and South. There was no news of those who remained initially. However after about three hours debris was falling down along with corpses of humans and animals... it continued for a while and then nothing.

...

Athlantic Ocean experienced high tides and moving Tsunamis, some of which swallowed up coastal areas.

Since all the habitation from the coastal region had been relocated, the damage was minimal; thanks to excellent planning by Kalam, Levy and team and the prompt action by the concerned governments.

...

However it was a different story in South America. Jupiter had literally broke it into two pieces along lower Paraguay and upper Argentina. The huge chasm cutting across the entire continent swallowed up parts of Brazil, Paraguay, Uruguay, Argentina and Chile. The somewhat rectangular mass of land was sucked up into Jupiter with such speed that it was beyond what the scientists had predicted. Those who stayed there were mostly prepared with capsule houses, oxygen, miniaturised food and such other things in addition to communication equipment. However, there was no signal except from one source which was very weak... and soon... that too... disappeared. The sea flowed through the gash creating a new sea with few floating islands. The separated land mass to the south drifted farther away.

...

The Raul Conti stadium was sparsely packed. Though the area was declared safe, most of the people including footballers were either involved in evacuation operations or in some activity connected with the Jupiter transit. Yet there were few diehard football lovers who had come to witness the friendly match between Chile and Argentina. Gomez and Sebastian were the main strike force of Argentina. The game was goal less till the first 34 minutes. Then the Chilian right half Claudio was fouled by Kempus. Claudio was a master of the 'Carlos Kick' which he had modified to his own style. He kicked the ball to the left... it arched to the left of the goal post and continued arching beautifully beating a surprised goal keeper and three jumping defenders and entered the goal at the right end! The crowd went into ecstasy at the beauty of the kick. They roared. Gomez was among the headers trying to head the ball... Sebastian was in the centre hoping to exploit the opportunity if the defenders reflected it. The crowd roared... suddenly there was a sound of crack... the ground behind Sebastian caved in swallowing all the players on the Argentinian goal side and the spectators on that side. A long canal...zigzag... earth rolling as if being pushed and pulled from up and down...it was so sudden that there was no indication whatsoever! Since it was supposed to be a safe area even the government hadn't paid much attention. It was all over in a few minutes. A 200 to 300 meter wide and more than two kilometre long cut passing through the ground took many lives, buildings, livestock and much more. From somewhere water rushed along with live bodies of humans and animals struggling for breath... corpses and debris... all were quiet. The nature returned to normal as if nothing happened. The players and spectators recovered from the shock and resorted to rescue action. Sebastian called aloud with tears rolling over his cheecks, "Gomez...!" Many others called many other names... one odd answer came... rest swallowed up by the unknown. By the next morning the southern portion of the Chasm was floating away with the lower part of S America in a south western direction.

...

"Oh! My God! Totally unexpected" Levy said and so did Kalam. Such unexpected things were happening in few other places too. However, Kalam was more worried about the exit of Jupiter. Unless it turns half a degree more in response to the last few pods and Cyclones it will cause much more damage. He was glued to the screen looking through 'Big Eye' observatory-the biggest telescope in space placed recently by ISRO in collaboration with Japanese. It was manned by a mixed team headed by Raziya Iyer.

"Could you measure it, Raziya?"

"You won't believe it Kalam... there is someone else up somewhere... the giant had moved almost one degree... I don't know how!"

"What... One degree !!!" He controlled his excitement and said, "Raziya check it again... be sure... we don't have super human powers, memsab"

"Sure as my head!"

"Thanks... I hope most of the space crafts are in its orbit by now" He heaved a sigh. It was a big relief. In another week Earth will be totally clear of Jupiter's effects and they can concentrate more on assessing the damage in detail and restoring whatever possible.

* * * * *

CHAPTER 13

Levy had a tough job but he was happy that most of the relief camps were functioning well and help was pouring in from all over the world. The people from regions unaffected were so generous that the donations in cash and kind were overflowing. Voluntary Service organisations were working along with Disaster Management and Relief organisation of UN. The rains, quakes, tsunamis and such other natural calamities had reduced though not stopped completely. Even the weather was clearing up.

The world map had been redesigned by Jupiter. It was still in the process of finalising. A number of island were still floating... most of them new ones. Many areas have submerged into the sea. The shape of the seven seas itself had undergone alteration.

The southern part of Africa and South America were still moving down. The Arctic ice was melting faster than expected. Many other glaciers all over the world were also melting at different rates flooding the rivers in many countries. India had mild floods in Ganges and Brahmaputhra while in Shyok river the flood was severe. Most of the Southern part of North India and down generally remained normal except for some quakes, landslides and cyclones. The government was able to control the damages effectively. India's DRF Teams (Disaster Relief Teams) were the best in the world and were directing rescue and relief operations all over the world.

Kalam and Levy had foreseen this situation and has planned in detail to ensure an orderly survival without panic. They had done it in phases. Damage assessment, despatching of technical teams, followed by Command & Administration teams, organising Local Administration Committees and lastly handing over administration to new governments or existing ones.

It was a month after Narayanan said, "we are nowhere". Now they were somewhere in Indian ocean. Pieces of landmasses coming from many directions had joined together to form a new mini continent... almost the size of Australia. Though they were people from different countries suddenly they felt that they belonged to a Newformed Land. The people who were there began to move around and make friends. Levy had sent a number of technical teams with equipment and established some new communication towers and repair the existing ones. In a few days they were able to communicate on certain general frequencies. The buildings which had solar power like that of Narayanan's house could operate electrical and electronic equipment. It was a big relief as some news about the world could be seen by people. The UN Command and Administration teams too had landed on many such areas to coordinate the administration in these new islands. The world was surviving the calamity without any panic and doing it so with a firmness and dedication as speedily as possible. The planning done beforehand by Kalam and Levy bore fruit now as there was no panic anywhere. The world over had faith in these two men. They were considered as the messengers of God even by erstwhile jihadis and terrorists.

However the prediction for the future was not that prospective. The world was to face a severe and prolonged winter which was going to prolong in certain areas for ever. Gradually the habitable space would reduce. Foreseeing this, the scientists had already developed variety of food which can be grown without soil, cloned livestock and such innovations. The speed of earth's rotation was slowing down due to which the ice cover and darkness were to envelope many parts of the world in due course. Since these predictions were already known, most of the countries had prepared underground cities drawing energy from the core of earth. The system was first developed in DRDO of India which they used in Siachen glacier. Its success prompted other nations to adopt and develop the technology. India never took patent for it saying that it is for the good of the humanity. Different countries developed many accessories for underground living without taking any patent. The science and technology was shared for the common good of the world following the lead from India... "Loka samastha sukhino bhavanthu"

Kalam had his establishment over and under the ground. They generally functioned from outside only, the underground manned by a skeleton staff. They expected to move down only in next century... that too,... if required!

It will take few months before any signal from anyone... IF!

Prithviloka

"At last... Arye, we have done it!" Vajrasimhan announced triumphantly. He had ensured that none of the rearguards of Bruha's force caused any damage to Prithvi. Further he was in contact with Thejaswiny in Deerghamandala. She was directing most of the pieces of Prithvi into this. Deerghamandala already had some traces of water and vegetation and a compatible atmosphere. On orders of Pritha she had enhanced them all. One of the captured soldiers of Bruha mentioned that Bruha was planning to cut off Deerghamandala with portions of Prithvi to float and move towards the Thamogartham. Bruha had a feeling that Deerghamandala is a cursed piece and it was cause of all his problems. Pritha, Thejaswiny and Vajrasimha had concluded that Bruha will cut off Deerghamandala as soon as he is on the verge of the Thamogartham. He will clear Bruhaloka leaving Deerghamandala to float towards the Thamogartham. Pritha had decided to keep quiet until then, then pull it out and keep it near her so that she can build upon it later. They made sure that the plan remains a secret so that Bruha does not change his plans. However in case Bruha had other plans Pritha had decided to cut off Deerghamandala step by step without alerting Bruha. Either way she was ready.

"I have taken most of the pieces there. It is strange that many of them have species on it huddled in some sort of caves." Thejaswini said. "Further there are some vimanas coming towards it... few of them have gone elsewhere. Those which are coming towards it, I am blowing them into it..."

"Excellent! I am looking at it this way, we are getting an upagruha with developed species in it... makes our work easier"

They all were surprised and amazed at the way the species performed. Never ever has it ever happened so in the history of the Cosmic Universe.

"Thejaswini,," said Pritha. "Host them well... In a while we will move the Prithvi or whatever left of it also to it and create a new Prithvi!"

Guruloka

"So now we are on our own... no interference from anyone" Bruha roared triumphantly.

"Yes! Bhagavan... though we lost Pushkara."

"Lost is lost, let us think of future. First things first, cut off Deerghamandala and push it towards Thamogartha as we pass by it. Plan to..."

Bruha gave out the detailed plan to establishing his realm in the new area. He felt that he should have had a chance to inflict more damage to Prithvi... but ruefully envied the way she manipulated herself out of his reach.

"I am the Aditya here! Ha! haaa!" he said in his mind. He told his ministers and chieftains,

"Let us celebrate it!!!"

Aditya loka

Today both Chaya Devi and Sandhya Devi were present in the Sabha. Aditya, as usual looked brilliant and majestic. He addressed the Supreme Council.

"I am happy to formally announce that Bruha has left us and forming his own Sourayootham. It is a powerful one with about 40 or more Upagruhas. We will keep a close watch over them so that they do not try any misadventures against us. I admire and appreciate Pritha. She has not only avoided Bruha but also created a new Prithvi where her species will continue to grow. This is the first time a species had created their own Gruha... amazing indeed! I give her my blessings and whatever help she needs".

Both the ladies though appreciated it, nevertheless... had a bit of reservation it appeared... natural feminine feeling.

Bhrahmaloka

"Pritha has done it! She has obtained her revenge of Pushkara, yielded some damage to Bruha and gained some" said Narada.

"Brilliant" said Parvathy.

"So now we have another Aditya in Bruha and a new Prithvi soon" said Mahadev. "Vishnu will have some additional work"

"I feel Ma Parvathi should enter the species – Devyani" said Narada.

"I don't think so… she appears to be immensely capable… Pritha and Thejaswini are there to guide her" Parvathy said.

"I think she is right" Mahadev said. "Maharshi, we are witnessing a new epic… enacted by the species, for the first time"

"Yes, Mahadev… I agree with you"

Earth June 2045

The world was relieved at the final announcement of exit of Jupiter by J QUEST, India. However the commotion and troubles were far from over. The cosmically redesigned earth had to come to terms with the new islands and broken continents. Levy and his team were at it. The UN had gained strength and approval from all the quarters for their effort and Mr John Onkarabile was unanimously re-elected as chairman for another term. India has risen to the top… it has become the World Leader in every sense. Indian spirituality had begun to spread like a new religion people adopting Sanathan Dharma as the religion of the world. There was a reign of peace… at least for the time being.

All observatories were listening all the 86400 seconds... for a beep...crackle...blip... anything! There were false alarms too from various quarters. However Kalam was patiently impatient.

In the Spaceship named EINDHOVEN, the one from Netherlands the robot Tosca could 'see' an atmosphere like area. The gases and fog like clouds were thick... yet she sensed Oxygen! It was miles away from Jupiter yet, was progressing at a good rate. The orbit had altered without its being aware. It was bewildered. Suddenly it felt a jerk and the speed increased alarmingly. As trained Tosca began adjusting speed to controllable levels. The fuel in the ship had remained stable... It saw huge formations of gases thick at first... gradually becoming light. It was 46 hours after the first jerk that the craft came under its control. Being a machine it could not heave a sigh of relief! Its sensors were sensing the presence of a wide variety of known gases and many new ones. It did some fast calculations... it was in the right orbit. At the rate at which it was progressing it should reach the Sea of Tranquility in another 16 plus hours. Tosca looked at the pods... time is closing!

On the farthest manned pod which have now become 'Giant 9', Talia the Israel born Captain of the Pod could hear a faint 'beep'! She was instantly alert and so was her crew of four, two men and two women from different countries. Talia was in her late thirties, roughly good looking, stern with an athletic physique. She was a peasant by birth and later came into space science and space walks with NASA and ISRO.

"Sandra, you hear that?!"

"We all did... where did it come from?"

"Well... Hope I am not hallucinating"

"No Talia, I heard it very clearly... said Ahmed"

"Sandra, turn on the IST (Intense sonic Tracker) and try tracking it"

"Am already on it... but nothing... "

"Hope it comes again!"

......

Tosca flipped the switch and gave a signal once more... it will keep repeating every 30 seconds. The ship was closing in on Jupiter slightly earlier than expected due to its altered orbit. However there were gas formations blocking the signal. It was in the dark for yet another few hours... suddenly it emerged from the huge column of gas cloud and was 'surprised' to find an atmosphere! It flipped the switch of the commander of the ship, Jhon Rembrant (a descendent of the artist's family). The waking serum entered his veins and he felt alive. Rembrant opened his eyes and breathed... he took a deep breath and clicked the switches which opened his pod. He gingerly sat up and looked at Tosca.

"Hi, Tosca! Goedendag!"

"Good day to you Commander… we seems to be nearing the target area"

"What!!!" he just couldn't believe that he was alive. He had lost the sense of time, there was a difference in everything, weight, breathing… ! Suddenly he remembered Kalam telling them – 'take a deep breath thrice, ask your mind to calm down, look around and slowly like a child trying to take its first step…' He did just that and found himself completely under control. He thanked Kalaam in his mind and slowly got out of the pad and kissed Tosca. "Wake up others, I will assume Command".

He proceeded to the command room and sat in the chair… turned a few knobs here and there… switched a few switches and looked in front. He couldn't believe his eyes… He was just a few hours from the sea of Tranquility… it was a barren landscape with something like a waterbody covering the entire area with patches of different colours… somewhat like earth from the space! He had the urge to shout into the mike that they have arrived… but again the discipline ingrained by Kalaam… 'make sure you are there before you let us know… a whole world is awaiting… on tenterhooks'. His crew of eight and Tosca joined him. Each of them were on the verge of creating history… live or die… it will be in JUPITER!!!

The machines told them that there is an atmosphere outside which is safe. Yet they will not remove the space suit, nor the connecting tube... unless made sure. The ship kept going in the orbit smoothly... unbelievable. The signal was being transmitted... but no reply yet...

Now he could see the landscape... barren with clouds of a million colours... there were rock formations... desert like areas... dampness!

They passed a huge mountain with a channel... may be a dried up river...

It was all blue suddenly... like glass... waves and surf... a SEA!

The craft passed it and approached a barren area... the Sea Of Tranquility... yet no reply to any signal... "distance to land?" he asked Aleena.

"60 km... 50..."replied Aleena. Rembnrant took a deep breath and said, "taking manual control"

The craft slowed down gradually and became standstill at 20 km. He opened the landing thrusters... the craft slowly descended. Aleena kept announcing the distance as they went down... 30... 20... 10... five... he opened the balloons and parachutes... the craft slowed down further... three... two... one... 800 meters...500... the excitement was so much...400... 300... she had a lump in her throat... couldn't speak... yet managed... 200...100... the first space craft was just 100 meters from Jupiter!!!

He pinched himself... is it real!... Aleena's voice woke him 50... he steadied his hands and said into the microphone...

"Earth... we are touching down on Jupiter!"

The craft slowly, steadily extended its landing pods... as soft as a puss putting its paw...

LANDED !

It was 1526 HOURS GMT 18 SEPTEMBER 2046.

Rembrant spoke in full throated voice "Earth... this is Eindhoven... landed at Jupiter 1526 hours GMT 18 September 2046"

For a while no one spoke,... total silence except for the beep of the signal. Then all hell broke loose. They hugged each other including Tosca... tears unashamedly flowing down the cheecks!

Rembrant asked Tosca to intensify the signal beam... he knew that the distance has to be first ascertained. They had moved along with the main planet out of the Solar system. It took some time to fix the location. He ordered Tosca to align the communication antenna accordingly and send a pulse in the new frequency towards earth...

...

Giant 9 reported to Kalam about the faint beep. Kalaam closed his eyes and visualised Jupiter and the Sea of Tranquility. Suppose one of the spaceships had reached it... As per his calculations and that of the world it was supposed to happen only sometime in the early October.

"Track the present location of Jupiter" He told Talia and his own staff. They were already on it but were not able to ascertain yet. Talia was able to track it since their pod was the farthest in the Jupiter's exit route. As per that Sea of Tranquility appeared to be in a different angle which blocked its signal from earth.

"Kalaam I am manoeuvring to a position and will try to receive... if possible"

"Yes, do that... he said with full of hope"

...

"Tosca, keep trying. Cameroon, open the outer hatch..."

"Outer hatch opening" Cameroon and the landing crew studied the dials and said "... extending feeler cords" a snake like wire with a small hood extended outside till it touched the ground. It was hard sand, rocky pebble like...presence of various gases including oxygen! There was a slight wind, the temperature outside was a bit hot... around 34 degrees.

"Open inner hatch"

"Inner hatch opening"

"Landing crew ready"

Ludwig was the first one, he was a 41 year old German engineer specialised in space walk and repair. He had worked with Devyani too. He was followed by Catherine the 38 year old French astrophysist. She too was an experienced space walker. Ludwig slowly raised his head (hood) out of the hatch and carefully looked around... "all clear"...

"Proceed"

He moved up gingerly holding on to the railing with the umbilical cord in place... one feet on the ladder... second... third... just one step away from history!

...

Talia completed the manoeuvring very carefully and switched the intensifier... it should come... nothing...yet...

"...rtrrrrrrrrrrrrrrrrrr...hingzzzzzzzzzzzzzzzz..."

"Lost! Hope it is not something of my imagination" Talia said.

"IT'S COMING AGAIN" Sandra said with full excitement of a school girl. They all listened...

"...Einhorrrrrrrrrrr...nded on Jupzzrr......... September 2046" Some adjustments of the communication frequencies tuned the system to both the senders and receivers. Talia tried to speak... she couldn't... her eyes welled and overflowed... a lump in the throat... Sandra took over the mike and spoke in clear spaced words. "This is Giant 9, Eindhoven, I presume... we, the Earth is thrilled to know that you have landed in Jupiter"

Unlike the well controlled person he was, Kalaam jumped from his chair like a frog jumping... to the surprise of all. He shouted... "Eindhoven landed on Jupiter !"

Entire world repeated it in a million languages... a million voices. People cried, shouted, embraced, kissed... a world gone mad literally. In Netherlands, Germany and France people went hysterical. Emily Rembrant, an ardent Buddhist sat in front of the small statue of Buddha with folded hands with her four children close to her... tears flowing down her cheeks,

"Oh! Buddha, protect him"

...

Ludwig gingerly extended his feet till it stepped firmly on the ground... He said "first step in Jupiter". Carefully he put the second and third and fourth. "It's like Earth may be a bit lighter... Catherine, come" Catherine too stepped on the ground. It was firm, they shook hands and embraced and flashed the V sign.

Now Rembrant and crew stood in front of the camera with their thumbs up. Rembrant said calmly and firmly,

"Yes Earth, we are here alive... on Jupiter!"

It took another few days for other crafts to arrive. Some were lost. Thrishanku arrived on the second day just 16 hours after Eindhoven. Most of the crafts had landed in an area of around 40 earthly kilometres while few had landed far away. However all of them were in communication with each other. They had been instructed that no one should remove the space suit before Thrisanku permits them to. Devyani and her landing crew carried out a number of mandatory test and found that the atmosphere had plenty of oxygen... even few droplets of water. She was the first one to open the hood of her suit, a breeze of cool and warmth touched her as if welcoming. Slowly others followed suit. C'men released the nanoised air taxi. It was de – nanoed to the original size, a small rocket car. Two of the crew were sent on an observation recce flight which covered a distance of approximately 3000 kms. What they saw and some samples collected surprised everyone. There were some pieces of real earth probably from those land masses sucked in by Jupiter. There was a leaf too with a cocoon of butterfly!... life throbbing in it.

In the next few days Devyani and her command team roamed around in their space taxi and established contact with Rembrant and all other Commanders. They were told to extend their area as much as possible to avoid cluttering. She wanted to cover the entire area but Kalam advised her not to. He instructed her to first establish a Control Head Quarters under C'Men and have a council with people from some of the ships. The five regions were divided with Thrisanku in the Center and the five regions developing into five petals. The atmosphere was fast becoming habitable with algae, some plants, bushes and vegetation coming up. They had two rains and after that the rivers formed flowing into the sea.

* * * * *

CHAPTER 14

Future

The landmasses with its adamant inhabitants who had stayed with it had experienced something unimaginable and unforgettable. First few months they were asleep... then some of them started waking up. Kulwanth was one of the early risers.

When he opened his eyes he felt tired and shaken. He looked around... yes, all those who started were still there. He gingerly stood up holding a chair for support. 'Breath in... and out... repeat... and repeat' he remembered his Yoga Teacher Iyangar saying. After performing pranayamam for three times he felt some control over his mind and body. He moved to the front cabin of the Igloo without disturbing others. It had a periscope connected with it. He slowly adjusted the knobs. The camera lens slowly revolved clockwise. Kulwanth couldn't believe. They have not moved... the landscape was almost the same as it was when they went to sleep except for some dust and snow. He had a temptation to do a 'bhangda'. However, he remembered what Kalaam had instructed all. "Keep the mind under your control". He moved inside the igloo to control his movements... felt a bit heavier. No this was not earth... once again he scrutinised the view through the periscope... it was unfamiliar... it seemed. He could breath! He woke up others. All were in a state of stupefied amazement... to believe that they are alive! Each of them took their turn at the periscope and couldn't make out anything. Harjinder spoke to everyone.

"We will see outside… come what may!"

In an hour's time all of them were ready.

Harjinder said "Vah gurujika khalsa vah Guruji ka fatheh… Bole sonihal sat sri akaal… Nalini, open the door"

Nalini opened the door and Harjinder stepped out of the house into the garden of their house. It was there… intact… lot of ice flakes lying there… they were already melting. His cattle and the tractor, the other vehicles… all were there. His whole family, livestock and the vehicles were there. He thanked Vahe Guru in his mind. Visibility was more or less a haze; he could see no Sun. In the dimlight he could see the silhouette of the landscape… not much has changed. He asked Kulwanth to open the transmitter and try to establish communication on the unified frequency Kalaam had given them. Kulwanth switched the screen also along with the transmitter. He sent a drone into the 'sky'.The drone went up and stabilised at 500meters. Kulwanth could see shadows moving here and there in all directions. He was scared. He said stammering… "Papa… something…"

Manpreeth sensed the alarm and looked carefully into the screen and almost screamed.

"There is Bharadwaj uncle!!"

"WHAAAAAT!!!" They all looked into the screen and yes... it was Bharadwaj, a schoolmate of Harjinder who told him before they parted, "Bhai Harry, meet you on Jupiter"

...and here they were!

Harjinder couldn't speak for a while. Then suddenly he ran out... as if mad and called out loudly "Paradwaaj". He walked another hundred yards or so when the figure emerged out of the door covered with ice. "Tho thoo bhi pahunch gaya?" (So you also arrived?)

They embraced and soon there were others. The block which carried them had about ten families scattered here and there. One was lost along with a portion of their land. Rest of them all the nine were alive and well, making it a population of about 30 humans and few animals cows, dogs, cat and horses. Three tractors, few cars and few two wheelers were also there. The buildings and ground were almost intact except for ice and miner damages. Even the vegetation was intact. They could breath, though with some difficulty. Beyond the block of earth they could see a brown desertish expanse of land with few bushes and trees. Cool breeze was present... somewhere it was raining... the bird, insect and animal life was just waking up. Kulwant could establish communication with Thrisanku and later through them to back home,... earth.!

...

There were many such others from different parts of the world scattered over the Sea of Tranquility. When

C'Men and his team finished the search they could observe a total of area almost the size of Brazil scattered all over. In most of them life was thriving. Communication was through with all of them and they did take a census on the spot. When compared with the data from earth they found that at least 60 percent of the land that was pulled out by Jupiter and its moons had survived with miner damages. The region had vegetation of a primitive level, mostly shrubs and bushes-small channels where something like water was flowing... the water tasted different. The ground was harder than that of the earth. There were clouds too scattered over the sky. The landmasses that had been taken in by Jupiter were almost intact with their manmade structures, flora and fauna, animal life... all in a limbo... as if captured in amber... but of a different nature. Most of them were still alive!

However there was a difference... there was no Sun or Moon... stars were there... different constellations that were hitherto unknown... as if they were looking at some different galaxy.

"Can you give us an idea... where are we...?" Devayani asked Kalaam.

Kalam had already tracked them into a region somewhere between Andromeda and Milky Way galaxies. That was the reason why they were viewing different constellations. Earth could only communicate with them but no visual images could be obtained for some unknown reason. The time lag also was more. However, Earth was happy that a majority of the people and landmass had survived and landed in Jupiter. From the reports received from them the prospect of survival was very much positive. The atmosphere and the environment in the S o Ty was fast becoming habitable... sufficient oxygen was present... so was water... no sunlight but yet there was some light, like a bright moonlight... Could be the light from Jupiter.

What will be their future...!

Down on Earth, Levy and his team was battling tremendous odds... to control and realign the floating pieces of islands, rather reshape the world itself. It took almost four months to survey the earth. The Northern Hemisphere had undergone minor alterations only; some craters in Canada, Greenland, Russia, etc. The middle too did not alter much except that the gap between North and South America had widened and few islands disappeared. It is the Southern hemisphere which really suffered. The African continent had been clearly cut into two, the southern portion had floated around 100 kms south closing towards Antarctica. So was South America; the portion below northern Argentina had been split and the southern portion moving down towards Antarctica. The oceans had created havoc by rushing into the land/ flushing out towns and villages out of the land. The damage was irreparable. However the world over was taking part in a mega rescue and resettling operation on their own in addition to what Kalam and Levy were doing.

It was an year before some semblance of stability could be achieved. The reorganised earth looked vastly different from what the world knew. A huge crater had slashed through Canada and NE USA, Russia too had a similar canyon starting from the Siberian deserts going towards Khazakisthan. Another canyon ran across North China extending all the way down to Punjab of India and going further down to the sea through Pakisthan. Africa and South America had been cut into two and the southern portions had moved closer to Antarctica. The waters had covered more portions of the earth and the snow cover had started melting bringing more water into the oceans. The weathermen had predicted a gradual winter which will prolong and keep going on and on covering the entire earth in a not-so-distant future. Kalam had identified regions which may remain clear of ice and accordingly the scientific community had advised construction of underground cities. Many countries like Russia, USA, Germany, India, etc had already developed some such functional complexes. As and when the freezing begins they will shift into them. World was going from the 'Ultra Modern' to 'Cave dwellings'... As they say, 'the circle will complete'.

By the new year of 2050 things had almost become normal.

...

2056

In a humble looking villa in the outskirts of Lonavla a man was watering the flowers in his garden. He was in his mid sixties, lean and athletic with a crown of unruly hair. He was humming an old hindi song...

'... Jadon ki narmiyon ko angan me let kar... '

Kalam never felt happier. He was now the holder of 'Einstein Chair' the topmost honour for a scientist, Nobel and a variety of other such awards. For the world he was an incarnation. He had his office next to the residence on a small hillock from where communication was clear. He functioned from there, occasionally travelling to NASA or Genoeva and frequently to Space Stations. He had just returned from the farthest outstation in Space which was the transit for SoTy. Earth could not get the communication from SoTy instantly... there was a time lag... hence this station was the relay.

The news from Devyani was very encouraging; they had established a democratic form of government under C'men and were functioning very well. The atmosphere had become habitable so fast that Devi felt there is some supernatural force helping them. "Someone want us to settle down and flourish here... the nature, flora and fauna... all just like earth... that too so fast. This looks like the earth before modernisation started... wonderful"

"Try to keep it like that and do not spoil it"

Just then he heard a childish voice, 'mama, where is my pudding?' He suddenly said, "Huh?"

"Oh! She is two years now and I am carrying!"

Kalam cried... he shouted "Maya, come here" Maya was too happy to hear it. She already had two girls. But the Jupiter children was something. They conversed animatedly about many things like ladies do. Jupiter had not affected the gender behaviour much... it seemed.

Kalam said to himself... "The earth in Jupiter is... at last... generating!"

* * * * *

Epilogue

Few years then on, earth started freezing. The underground cities survived. Earth had colonised Moon, SoTy and one more new planet. The space stations in the outer space had become Space Cities. Human nature had not undergone much change because rivalries were already starting to show its effects. The technology was progressing at such a fast pace that nothing could control it.

Kalaam was cloned but it was more of a replica minus the mind. Try whatever, the humans could not clone the mind... probably the Gods would not have it. However, in the world they allotted the names Einstein and Kalaam for the top scientists alternatively. It was the tenure of Kalaam 3 now after three Einsteins.

In the SoTy, Devyani, C'men and the initial settlers had long gone by. Few generations had passed and the planet had developed into a mini earth with Continents and Oceans, wild life and nature, mountains and plains, countries and rivalries... Still somewhat different from the earth. Their time, day, night, seasons and monsoons were different from that of earth. It even affected their life span which was longer. Their intelligence surpassed that of any other known species. The SoTy gradually got cut off from Jupiter and was almost to be sucked into a black hole. However some force pulled it away and it became another satellite of the earth like moon. However as time went by it began to close towards earth.

Earth was completely frozen and except for few species caught in amber no sign of life existed there.

Bruha was told by his chief of Staff that they were near the Thamogartham. He ordered Deerghamandala to be cut off so that the Thamogartham will pull it into it. Deerghamandalam was cut off just at the periphery of the Thamogartham. It started floating towards the Gartham. Bruha smiled and said,

"At last...!"

Thejaswini and Bhavani also repeated it... "At last"

They had prepared chakravakams of a different nature; the 'Grahyam'. It could pull the Deerghamandalam into a vaccum and thereby bypass the Thamogartham and thereafter guide it towards Prithvi.

Pritha said with satisfaction. "Let them flourish there for a while, we will join them later. We will have our new species out of these itself..." She mentally thanked the species.

"A novel instance in the Sourayootham."

In due course Deerghamandala joined Prithvi. However the inhabitants of Deerghamandala found Prithvi as a ball covered almost fully by ice and some gases. Pritha took charge and ordered Thejaswiny to expand all over Prithvi.

3001

There were very few areas on earth which was still not frozen. The Sea of Tranquility was going to be the new earth. Once it joins the terra firma most of the remaining population from the unfrozen portion of earth would be shifting into it. The arrangements had already been made and co-ordinated between Earth and Sea of Tranquility.

... Kalam 3 watched Sea Of Tranquility closing in to Earth from his underground Head Quarters. It joined Earth after six months. A sophisticated space module landed just outside the Operational Headquarters of Earth. A human like figure emerged from it. Kalam, the PM of India and the UNSG were waiting at the open air field.

"Dr Kalam?" the figure addressed him.

"Yes... Maheswar, I presume".

"Yes Sir, On behalf of Sea Of Tranquility as representative of the Government I offer my greeting to you, the PM and UNSG".

"Welcome to Earth, you are no more part of Jupiter... you are The Earth" the PM said.

"Yes sir" said Maheswar. "We are happy to be... Earth,

... THE NEW EARTH!"

XXXXXXXXXX